CANTERWOOD CREST

TAKE THE REINS

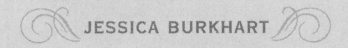 JESSICA BURKHART

ALADDIN MIX

New York London Toronto Sydney

This book is a work of fiction. Any references to historical events, real people, or real locales are used fictitiously. Other names, characters, places, and incidents are the product of the author's imagination, and any resemblance to actual events or locales or persons, living or dead, is entirely coincidental.

ALADDIN MIX

Simon & Schuster Children's Publishing Division

1230 Avenue of the Americas, New York, NY 10020

Copyright © 2009 by Jessica Burkhart

All rights reserved, including the right of reproduction

in whole or in part in any form.

ALADDIN PAPERBACKS, ALADDIN MIX,

and related logo are registered trademarks of Simon & Schuster, Inc.

Designed by Jessica Sonkin

The text of this book was set in Venetian 301 BT.

Manufactured in the United States of America

First Aladdin Paperbacks edition January 2009

21

Library of Congress Control Number 2008928592

ISBN-13: 978-1-4169-5840-6

ISBN-10: 1-4169-5840-1

0619 OFF

ACKNOWLEDGMENTS

Alyssa Eisner Henkin, my fab agent, you took a huge chance on me and I'm so grateful. You and the A-list rock! Molly McGuire, my former editor, thank you for giving Sasha and Charm a home. Kate Angelella, my supercool editor, thank you for taking this project and injecting it with your insight and limitless enthusiasm. Thank you to everyone at Simon & Schuster who worked on this book.

Jason, I ♥ our Mario Kart duels. (You don't have to admit that I won. A lot.) Thanks to my family, friends, and blog readers for letting me ramble (endlessly!) about my Canterwood world.

Em Hendricks, you kept me laughing. Ella Bográn, your support means so much. Emily Wilkinson, our wonderful childhood horsey adventures still inspire me. Pam Staton, you and AppleJacks gave me everything I needed for this book.

To my parents,

for giving me the best possible motivation.

1

OUR FANTABULOUS
ENTRANCE.
NOT.

MY PARENTS' SUV ROLLED INTO THE SCHOOL'S
parking lot, past the imposing, ivy-covered wrought-iron
gates. I had seven types of lip gloss in my purse and not
one was Canterwood Crest Academy worthy. Peach and
lime—too summery. Marshmallow and sugar cookie—
too Christmassy. Reluctantly, I settled on strawberry.

"Mom," I whispered, dabbing gloss on my lower
lip—desperate situations really amp up my lip gloss
addiction—"are you sure about this?" The rearview
mirror caught my reflection. My naturally tan face was
pale and I'd slathered on so many coats of lip gloss, my
lips had turned cotton-candy pink. Oops.

"You're going to be fine, Sasha. You were a great rider
at Briar Creek!" Mom turned in her seat to look at me.

She tucked a strand of golden-brown hair—the same color as mine— behind her ear.

I waved my hand toward the window. "*This* is not Briar Creek," I said, "I'll be lucky if I make the beginner team here."

"You're an excellent rider," Dad said, pulling into a parking space and cutting the engine. "Don't even talk like that."

Parents are required to say stuff like that so they don't ruin their kid's self esteem. I'd seen an *Oprah* about it.

I tried one of those deep-breathing exercises from my yoga DVD. In May, when my acceptance letter had come from school, I'd taken up yoga. The thought of switching schools and riding for a new stable had been enough to give me major stress. But I couldn't do any worse here than I had at UMS—Union Middle School—in my hometown of Union. Maybe I'd make real friends here. *Breathe in, and then out. In, out.*

"All right, Sash," Dad said. "Let's go."

Reluctantly, I opened the door and took in the scene around me. Everything looked different, bigger some-how, than when I'd toured the campus in April. Beautiful stone buildings with climbing ivy, rolling green hills, lush trees with not one dead leaf to be found. And, best of all, a gorgeous, dark-lacquered stable ahead in the distance.

"Smile! Say hi to Grandma and Grandpa, honey." Dad said, shoving his camcorder in my face. "This is Sasha's first day of seventh grade. Wave to the camera, Sasha."

"Dad!" I hissed. Oprah would so totally disapprove of this! I reverted to my yoga breathing. In, out. In, out.

He beamed. "Sasha's first day at boarding school. I remember when—"

Oh, my God. "Dad! Stop filming!" I slammed my palm over the lens. "Not. Now."

"Oh." Dad lowered the camcorder and switched off the blinking red light. "Sorry."

Mom read the instruction sheet for students coming to school with horses. "It says to unload your horse in this lot," Mom said. "And follow the signs to the stable area."

At least there were signs, since I probably wouldn't remember the way after five months.

Dad put away the camcorder and helped me unload my horse. Charm pawed the trailer floor—eager to get out. He had been in the trailer for two hours.

Charm, with nostrils flaring, backed down the trailer ramp. "Please behave," I whispered to him. He pranced in place and huffed as he eyed his new home. His chestnut coat glistened, his gold halter rings flashing in the sunlight. Charm was acting like a yearling instead of an eight-year-old gelding. I touched the tiny silver horse charm on the bracelet my parents had given me for good luck last night, our last night together before Canterwood.

"We'll go park the trailer and find you in the stable when we're done," Mom said.

"You're leaving me alone?"

"Oh, honey," Mom said, squeezing my shoulder. "You'll be fine. And we'll be right back."

"Promise?" I asked.

She nodded. "Promise."

My slick hands could barely grip Charm's lead line. Deep breath in, deep breath out. "Ready, boy?"

My lips felt dry. I dug in my pocket for my strawberry gloss and globbed more on. Together, Charm and I followed a sign that read STABLE, with an arrow that pointed down a grassy path. Iron signs directed riders to cross-country courses and trail riding paths. As we approached the stable, the familiar scent of horses, hay, and grain soothed me more than my breathing exercises or lip gloss ever would.

Wow, Canterwood is even more gorgeous than I'd remembered, I thought, surveying the gleaming paddocks. The lush grass looked as if someone had cut it with fingernail clippers. There wasn't a clump of horsehair or a wisp of hay out of place. Even the stones around the bushes by the sidewalks looked polished.

This place made Briar Creek look like a dollhouse-size operation. I still couldn't believe I'd been accepted to Canterwood and was about to start riding for their nationally recognized riding program!

Charm tugged me forward. "Easy," I murmured.

Just then, a *boom* came from the parking lot. At the same moment that I realized it had just been a car backfiring, my hand shot out to grasp Charm's halter. With a snort, he reared up toward the bright blue sky. The lead line seared my palms as it slipped out of my hands. I stumbled backward and made a frantic swipe for the end of the rope, but Charm bolted forward before I could grab it.

Oh, my God, this couldn't be happening! In the distance, I could see Charm's lead line dangling between his legs. He could seriously hurt himself if he got tangled in the rope.

"Charm!" I yelled, sprinting after him. He galloped toward a cluster of students and then swerved to avoid them. He flew by the paddocks and headed for the arena, his hooves pounding the ground in quick beats.

"Loose horse!" I screamed.

Charm's ears swept back in fear. The whites of his eyes were visible, even from far away. Charm quickened his pace to a flat gallop. Thirteen hundred pounds of glistening chestnut zoomed around the grass.

"Here, Charm!" He slowed to a fast canter and turned toward a much darker chestnut Thoroughbred in the arena. The horse's shoulder muscles rippled under his shiny coat. A slight girl with blond hair that peeked out from beneath a black velvet riding helmet was riding the Thoroughbred.

"Watch out!" I yelled to the girl. But if she heard me, she didn't show it.

Charm flew past the Thoroughbred and knocked over a row of orange cones lined up on the outside of the arena. A cone tumbled right into the Thoroughbred's path; he reared and stretched high into the air. For a second, it looked like he would tip backward onto the girl.

My breath caught. All I could do was stare. The girl flipped off her horse's back and landed in the arena dirt.

Oh. My. God.

This was my worst nightmare.

"Charm!" I almost didn't believe it when Charm finally slowed into a trot. I grabbed his lead line with shaking hands. His sides heaved and the whites of his eyes receded as he began to calm. I pulled him into the arena entrance, ignoring my burning palms. We ran over to the girl who hadn't moved since her fall.

"Oh, my God, are you okay?" I asked. Charm stood still next to me and lowered his head.

"Where's my horse?" the girl asked, her voice surprisingly strong for someone who had just had a serious fall.

"Right over there," I pointed. "He looks okay," I said, hoping that was true as I looked over to where he stood at the far end of the arena. The girl struggled to sit up.

"Wait," I said. "Should you sit up?"

The girl wiped dirt from her eyes.

"What can I do?" I asked.

"Just help me take off my helmet."

My trembling fingers unfastened her chin strap and I lifted the helmet from her head. "I'm so, so sorry. Please let me go get help." Out of the corner of my eye, I saw a dark-haired girl duck under the fence and grab the Thoroughbred's reins.

"Mr. Conner is coming, Heather," she said, leading the Thoroughbred. Charm lifted his head to eye the new horse, who stood quietly and peered down at his rider.

"Thanks, Callie," the blonde—Heather—said.

"Did you hurt anything?" Callie asked.

Heather wiggled the fingers on her left hand. "This arm."

"Is Heather's horse okay?" I asked Callie.

Callie's dark brown eyes flickered over Heather and then toward me. She felt the horse's legs. "I don't feel any heat. Aristocrat seems fine to me."

My old instructor, Kim, had taught me that, too. If Callie felt any heat, Aristocrat could have sprained or pulled something.

"Thank God," Heather moaned. "We have a show in a month."

"Thank you so much for grabbing him!" I said to Callie. "I can't believe that happened on my first day!"

A tall man with thick, dark hair strode over. I recognized him immediately from the Canterwood Crest Academy website: Mr. Conner, my riding instructor. And he definitely wasn't happy.

"What happened?" he asked, kneeling down to check on Heather.

"My horse got loose, sir," I confessed, my voice shaky. "He spooked and I couldn't hold onto him."

"Who are you?" Mr. Conner asked, raising his eyebrows.

"Sasha Silver. I'm new this year." I wondered if I would set a school record by getting expelled on my first day.

Mr. Conner felt Heather's arm from her shoulder to her fingers. "Nothing feels broken. But let's get you to the nurse, Heather, just to make sure."

Heather clutched her right arm. "It hurts, Mr. Conner."

Mr. Conner motioned to Callie. "Callie, please take Aristocrat back to the stable, untack him and be sure he's fed."

"Yes, sir," Callie said. "I saw what happened. It really *was* an accident."

I mouthed a silent *thank you* to Callie and she smiled in return before leading Aristocrat out of the arena.

"I'm feeling kind of dizzy," Heather said. "Could I sit for one more second?"

"Of course," Mr. Conner said, kneeling beside her. "Take a few deep breaths."

What if she had head trauma? How could I tell Mom and Dad that in the ten minutes they left me alone, this happened? No way would yoga breathing be enough to calm them down if I got expelled my first ten minutes at Canterwood.

"Were you not taught how to control a spooked horse?" Mr. Conner asked. "You're not here to learn the basics."

I couldn't believe this! First days were for good impressions. Charm and I had been practicing harder than ever lately. We'd worked all summer on form and jumping—sometimes thirty hours a week.

"It happened so fast," I said. "I wasn't able to catch him."

Charm shifted his weight and his ears drooped. Mr. Conner helped Heather to her feet. When they started walking, I noticed she wasn't clutching her arm anymore.

"I expect you and your horse to be on your best behavior for the rest of the week, Ms. Silver," Mr. Conner called back over his shoulder.

I exhaled. "Noises like that never scare you, Charm," I whispered. "What happened?" Charm blinked and gave me his trademark sad puppy eyes. "We caused trouble in our first fifteen minutes, boy. Not a good start." He lowered his head. "It's all right. Let's go find your stall."

Charm and I approached the stable entrance when a girl with curly hair asked, "New rider, right?"

I nodded. "I'm Sasha and this is Charm."

"I'm Nicole Allen," the girl said. She patted Charm's shoulder. "Don't worry about it," she whispered. "No one will remember this tomorrow."

"Do you know where I should take Charm?" I asked her, recognizing an ally.

"I'll show you," Nicole said. Charm and I followed her into the stable.

I tried not to compare Canterwood to Briar Creek once I was inside the stable's main aisle—it felt disloyal. But this place was even nicer than the National Equestrian Club we had visited in Washington, D.C.! The aisles here were wide, the stalls were enormous, and no one was riding in jeans. I almost did a double take when I saw "Charm" on the gleaming gold nameplate on the stall door. The box stall, with light wooden boards, looked brand-new.

"I've got to go practice," Nicole said. "But I'll see you later."

Charm sniffed his new blue water bucket and lipped a few pieces of hay from the hay net. I fumbled in my pocket for my pink cell phone and pressed speed dial four.

"Hello?" Kim said.

"I haven't even been here a full half hour," I croaked into the phone. "And I've already humiliated myself."

"No," Kim said, her voice soothing. "What happened?"

"Charm got loose," I said.

"Oh, dear," Kim said.

"He spooked another horse and a girl fell."

Kim gasped. "Was she hurt?"

"Yes. No! I don't think so. She walked away on her own, but she was leaving for the infirmary."

"That doesn't sound too serious," Kim soothed. "It's only the first day. By tomorrow, something else will happen and no one will remember that Charm got loose. Believe me."

"I don't know," I said, as Charm started to nose my boot. I couldn't be mad at him when he looked so scared. He was new, too, and probably afraid of his new home. "Maybe I should have stayed at Briar Creek."

"Sasha, I loved having you here, but I taught you everything I could. We both know you want to grow as a rider."

"I know," I said quietly.

"I'm so proud of you, Sasha. And you can call me any-time you need to talk. Okay?"

"Okay," I agreed. "Thanks, Kim," I added, and said good-bye.

Charm nudged my back and I threw my arms around him. "It's going to be okay," I soothed. "We can do this." I reached under his jaw and tickled his hairy chin the way he liked. Charm flapped his lower lip up and down. It made a suction sound when it hit the top of his mouth. I laughed. "Thanks, boy. You always make me feel better."

"Sasha?" Mom called from behind the stall door. "Wow! This is such a nice space for Charm."

"I know, isn't it incredible?" I asked.

Dad glanced at me sideways. "You look upset. Everything okay?"

If I was going to make it, I couldn't be crying to my parents about every little thing. "Everything is fine. I'm just excited to see the dorms."

"Let's go, then!" Dad said.

2

WINCHESTER A.
BUTKIS HALL

I HAULED MY BAGS UP TO WINCHESTER A.
Butkis Hall.

That's right: Butkis. It was the worst hall name in
history.

All of the halls were named after famous Canterwood
graduates—Reynolds, Yule, and Hollis. Those names
conjured up images of senators and stony college campuses.
I had been stuck with Winchester A. Butkis residence hall.

"Need some help?" A girl with mousy hair peeked
her head out of a room labeled DORM MONITOR'S
HEADQUARTERS.

"Hi," I said, "I'm Sasha. Are you the dorm advisor?"

"Yes, I'm Livvie Davis." She had on a gray suit jacket
and neatly pressed khaki pants. Her face, pale and smooth,

would be even prettier with a dab of lip gloss. I looked around her immaculate office. A tin of newly sharpened pencils, a foot-high stack of paper and a black laptop filled the desk. A word-of-the-day desk calendar had a red circle around Friday and "move in" was written on the page. A clay jar with a "Just Study!" logo on the lid sat beside her lamp.

"That's cute." I said, reaching to touch the jar.

"Oh!" Livvie cried. "Don't—"

I yanked my hand back and looked at her, surprised. Oops. Was I going to mess up *everything* today?

"My paper clips are in there," Livvie said, as if that explained everything. She picked up the jar, set it down out of my reach, smoothed her sleeves, and smiled. "It took *forever* to arrange them by color and size."

I started to laugh at her joke, but realized that she was serious. About paper clips.

"I'll show you to your room. Your roommate, Paige Parker, moved in a couple of days ago. She's probably around here somewhere."

Paige and I had chatted on the phone two weeks ago. She was a seventh grader like me and it was her second year at Canterwood. Over the phone, Paige told me she knew exactly what we needed.

"Could you bring a microwave and minifridge?" Paige asked.

"Anything else?"

"I don't mind bringing all of the important stuff," Paige said.

Fingers crossed for a plasma-screen TV. "Like what?" I asked.

"Like lint brushes, a vacuum, bathroom cleansers, a good mop and broom. You know, things like that," Paige said. "My last roomie was a rider, so I know what it takes to keep a room fresh and allergen free." Her tone had been cheerful enough, but I'd wondered if she thought I was messy just because I was a rider.

Livvie led me toward my room, where Mom and Dad eventually caught up with us. Livvie dangled a silver key in front of my eye.

"Here is your dorm key," she said. "I'll be back in a little while to answer any questions about your orientation packet."

My fingers clutched the rough metal.

I stuck the key into the lock and turned it. The room was beautiful—spacious, with polished wood floors and furniture. There were two big windows with a gorgeous view of campus over each of our beds. Paige's bed, nestled under the second window, was directly across from mine. We each had a nightstand. Piles of books lined Paige's stand. She was definitely a reader, just like me. Even the closets were huge! The soft beige walls looked as if they'd been painted yesterday.

A small coffee table in the center of the room had a vase of dahlias in the center. A few magazines were piled neatly on the table. Paintings of the Eiffel Tower and a blooming orchid made the walls pop. Paige must have done this.

Mom and Dad shuffled inside the dorm, arms laden with containers and bags of supplies. Dad placed some plastic trunks on top of my bed beneath a curtainless window.

Mom and I put away clothes while Dad sat on the bed and rested a minute from carrying all the heavy boxes. In the closet, Paige's outfits hung neatly on the right side. My jeans and T-shirts looked a little sad next to Paige's designer labels. Belted dresses, a box of pointy high heels and at least two dozen ballet flats of every color filled Paige's half of the closet. My metal shoe rack with my tennis shoes, boots, and flip-flops looked shabby next to Paige's shiny shoeboxes. My fingers skimmed the gold leather on one of the shoes. Size seven—like me. Maybe we could share! I knew Paige was from New York City—I hoped she wasn't a Manhattan fashionista who would mock my clothes.

While Mom and I finished the closet, I unloaded my study supplies onto my desk. Pink and purple were my choice pen colors, but Dad made me bring a couple of boring black and blue ones in case rainbow colors weren't serious enough for Canterwood. I hooked up my laptop and printer while Dad plugged in my electric blue desk light and stacked my notebooks next to the printer. It was looking more and more like my room.

"Excuse me, Silver family," Livvie said, popping her head in the dorm. "Sasha, I wanted to take a second to highlight the major rules before your parents leave."

"Okay," I said, sitting on my bed beside Mom and Dad.

Livvie took my desk chair.

"You've all read over the rules in the orientation booklet, right?" Livvie asked.

We all nodded. There were *so* many rules. When I'd gotten my orientation booklet in the mail a few weeks ago, I'd beeen so excited! But the more I read, the scarier everything seemed. Classes were known to be superhard at Canterwood—it was one of the best schools in the entire state of Connecticut. Back home, I had report cards filled with As. I worried that it might not be as easy to get those As here.

Livvie smiled. "Great! Then you already know that no boys are ever allowed in the dorms, you have to go to bed by ten thirty, and you have to keep a log of your study time. A half hour of studying is required each night per class. You'll turn in a study journal every Saturday."

Mom and Dad smiled at each other.

I tried to pay attention to what Livvie was saying, but my mind, and my eyes, wandered. Outside my window, a cute guy with a Zac Efron shaggy haircut walked down the sidewalk toward the parking lot. His sunglasses were nestled casually on top of his head. He grinned and slapped palms with a guy who passed him. I almost fell off the couch watching him.

"Finally," Livvie said, jarring me out of my ogling, "you'll have to give me notice and get permission in advance if you want to do anything other than regular Canterwood-approved activities." Livvie got up and shook Mom and Dad's hands. "Come see me if you have any questions."

"We will," Mom said. "Thank you."

"Let's grab your spare riding boots from the car before

we leave," Mom said. My stomach dropped. I didn't want to be reminded that they'd be leaving soon.

We left Winchester and in the parking lot, I spotted Heather a couple of cars away, standing next to a tall man.

"Your mother just told me about your report card!" the man, presumably her dad, yelled. His tone pierced my eardrums. He wore a suit. "Your grades will be better this semester or you're going home."

Heather glanced around. "I'll do better," she said.

Heather's dad yanked open the door of his car, got in, and drove out of the parking lot. The SUV's tires squealed and kicked up gravel.

Heather set her jaw and tilted her chin up.

"Hi," I called softly.

She looked at me and turned quickly, hurrying away.

Dad grabbed my boots from the backseat and handed them to me. I wrapped him up in a tight hug. "Thanks," I said.

"What for?" he asked.

"For being such a good dad."

He let me go and put an arm around my shoulder as we started to walk back toward Winchester Hall.

"Well, this is it," Mom said. "This is where we leave you."

"I'm a little nervous," I said. I tried to keep my voice even. I didn't want to start crying. "It's weird that you aren't meeting my teachers like you always do."

"It's perfectly normal to be nervous," Mom said, giving me a squeeze.

Dad's hazel eyes searched my face. "Remember, we got that plan so we can text, e-mail, and talk on the phone anytime you need us. And you'll be coming home for a long weekend soon."

"Right," I said. I thought of my cozy bed and familiar school back home. It was getting harder to stand there, knowing they were about to leave. I could already feel the heat behind my eyes. "Three weeks."

Mom gave me a final hug. "You'll be fine. We love you."

"I love you, too."

With a final wave, I turned back to my dorm room.

3

HOT BOY POSTERS
AND MAC 'N' CHEESE

INSIDE MY ROOM, A GIRL WITH LONG RED HAIR
and fair skin flipped through a glossy teen mag. She looked
up at me. "Sasha?" she asked.

I nodded. "Paige?"

Paige flashed a dazzling smile and perched on her bed,
the image of a Manhattan girl, dressed in black leggings
and a pair of ballet flats. "It's so nice to meet you! I came
two days ago to get the dorm ready for us. But my parents
and I had errands to run. Do you like the furniture place-
ment? If not, we can change it up."

"It looks great," I said. "I couldn't have made it look
this nice in two days."

Paige shrugged and rifled through her tan shoulder bag.
She pulled out a cereal bar. "Want one?"

"Sure, thanks."

"Organizing is my thing," she said. "I'm freakishly neat and if I have a kitchen to work in, I can't stop cooking or baking."

"Wow. I can cook mac and cheese, but that's it."

"I can teach you a few dishes sometime," she said. "If you want."

"That would be great." I looked at my wall and saw my bookcase still had an empty shelf. I pulled two seasons of *Southampton Socialites* out of my bag.

With eyes locked on the DVDs, Paige asked, "You're a fan?"

"All the way," I said, grinning. "I'm completely obsessed."

She nodded so hard her earrings rattled against her neck. "I've only seen a couple of episodes, but I love—"

"Hunter Miller!" I finished, laughing.

"Exactly!"

I wrapped my arms across my chest and sunk back into my pillow. "I also love *Tokyo Girls*, *Heaven's Kitchen*, and *Model Mania*. When I'm utterly bored, I'll watch *The Rose* or something mindless like that."

"You're so lucky," Paige said with a sigh. "I'm not allowed to watch TV at home. I only got to sneak a few episodes at my friend's house this summer."

"No TV? Really?" My jaw almost dropped.

"Really." Paige frowned. "I'm only allowed to watch educational stuff. My mom's on this learning-enrichment committee for our district, so that means no cable for the Parker household."

"I brought tons of TV shows on DVD. You can watch whatever you want."

Paige's face brightened. "That's so cool! The only DVD I brought was from a ballroom dancing competition from the eighties. My mom only has three thousand DVDs of those things."

"I love TV dancing shows," I confessed.

Paige finished her snack and pulled a box from under her bed. She dug around until she found a photo. In it, Paige was decked out in a flowing green gown, arm in arm with a tall guy in a tux as they did what appeared to be ballroom dancing.

"My mom makes me do ballroom dancing," Paige said. "I've been doing it for years. Once, I asked her if I could try salsa and she almost had a coronary. She thinks that Latin dancing is too sexy for me."

We burst into giggles.

"So," I said. "I happen to have a gorgeous poster of Hunter. Should we put it up?"

"Are you kidding? Get that thing up on the wall!"

Shoving a box aside, I dug in a container for the drool-worthy poster. I whipped it out with flourish and Paige handed me the tape.

"You do the honors," I said, bowing to her and Hunter in an I-am-not-worthy pose.

Paige put the last piece of tape on the wall and dreamy Hunter gazed at us—bronzed six-pack and all.

Paige stepped over to our tiny counter with two cabinets for snacks. We were allowed to have a microwave and minifridge, but that was it. We had to get permission if we wanted to cook in the dorm kitchen. The cabinets over-flowed with crackers, boxes of raisins, and packages of trail mix.

Paige gestured toward the cabinet. "My dad stocked this yesterday," she said. "He gets an awesome discount on all kinds of food since he runs a restaurant."

We settled on my bed, snacks between us, and began a chat session that took us through two *Southampton* reruns. "Why aren't you rooming with your old room-mate?" I asked.

Paige paused. "Well, Steph was supposed to make the intermediate riding team last year so she could try out for the advanced team this year. But she didn't ever get past the beginner level, so there was no way she could try out for the advanced team this year. It was so hard on her. She quit the team and transferred out of Canterwood."

"That's awful." My stomach flip-flopped. Is that what Paige would be saying about *me* next year? "So, what's the scoop on Canterwood?" I asked, eager to change the depressing topic.

Paige's eyes lit up. She twisted around to face me. "As I'm sure you've already heard, Canterwood has a long, long legacy of turning out Ivy Leaguers and famous equestrians. I'm here because of Canterwood's reputation for academic excellence—my mom really wants me to go to an Ivy. But because of Steph, I know a little about the equestrian scene here, too."

"Spill," I said. I paused the *Southampton* DVD and flopped back onto my pillow.

Paige reached for a bottle of pearly pink nail polish on her nightstand and began painting her nails as she talked. "This is only what I heard, so I can't be completely sure. But supposedly, the riding instructor Mr. Conner, is incredibly tough on his riders."

My stomach flipped again.

"There aren't many guys on the team, so you're going

to be competing against mostly girls. Girls like—" She stopped and looked away.

"Like what? What were you going to say?" I asked.

Paige bit her bottom lip. "Well, they're really competitive. Last year, this girl paid a rider's roommate to set back the girl's alarm clock so she'd miss the van leaving for the horse show."

"No way." My eyes widened.

"The girl got lucky, though. One of the other riders came over and woke her up, so she made it in time."

Whoa. Nothing like that had *ever* happened at Briar Creek. "Did the other girl get caught?"

"Well," Paige leaned forward. "Steph said the girl was caught by a teammate. The girl who caught her made her promise never to do anything like that again or she'd tell Mr. Conner."

"That was lucky. Hopefully, there aren't any girls here like that now. I had enough to deal with this morning."

"What happened?" Paige asked.

"Long story, but my horse got loose and knocked a girl off her horse."

Paige winced. "Maybe it wasn't as bad as you thought?"

"It was, unfortunately," I confessed. "I'm nervous

about the team meeting on Sunday. I test that day, too."

"What kind of test is it?" Paige asked.

"All of the new people have to ride for Mr. Conner. He'll decide if we ride for the beginner, intermediate, or advanced riding team. Apparently, there's a show next month, too. What if I'm not good enough?"

"If you're here," Paige said, "then you're good."

"I hope so." My voice sounded small. "But I guess I'll find out on Sunday."

We turned our attention back to Hunter and company. For the rest of the show, I couldn't concentrate. I took one of my deep yoga breaths. Sure, I could have stayed at Briar Creek, but there would have been no room to advance. Other riders would have moved up the ranks and I would have been stuck.

Now, I would be riding with the best. Canterwood was what I wanted.

Wasn't it?

Two hours and four *Southampton* episodes later, Paige sat up and stretched. "Are you hungry?"

"Starving," I said, stifling a yawn.

Paige checked her watch. "We usually have to go to the cafeteria, but it's not mandatory on Friday nights. I could whip up something in the dorm kitchen if we ask Livvie first."

"That sounds great!" It was official—I had the perfect roommate.

"Is grilled cheese and vegetable soup okay?" Paige asked.

"Perfect. I'll help."

We found Livvie in her office organizing her bookshelf. Classical music streamed softly from a CD player on the bookcase.

"Livvie?" Paige called, knocking on the open door.

"Hi, girls," Livvie said, barely looking up from her book pile. Her khakis were wrinkled and it looked like more paperwork had piled up on her desk.

"Is it okay if we make soup and grilled cheese sandwiches?" Paige asked. "I make them all of the time at home."

"Don't you want to go to the cafeteria?" Livvie asked. "It's not too late. If you go straight there and back, it's fine."

"Well . . . ," I started, not wanting to admit I was nervous about eating with a bunch of new people.

"I'd really love to make my grilled cheese for Sasha," Paige said. "You haven't had a real one until you've tried mine." She grinned at Livvie.

"Okay, okay," Livvie said. "But you'll have breakfast in the cafeteria tomorrow, right?"

"Right," I confirmed.

"Come get me if you need help." Livvie gave us a smile and turned back to her books.

Paige tossed the sandwiches in the pan and I stirred the soup.

"Do you know anyone here?" Paige asked, while we leaned against the counter and waited for the food.

"Nobody. It's a little scary."

Paige flipped the grilled cheese. "I can introduce you to some of the other girls on the floor and we can go to breakfast together tomorrow if you want."

"I'd like that," I said, stirring the soup faster.

I flipped open my phone and went to my photo album. "That's Charm." Charm, looking right at the camera, sparkled in the sunlight.

"Oh, he's adorable!" Paige grinned at the picture. "I wish I had a horse. Mom and Dad wouldn't even let me get a puppy, so they started giving me plants. My room at home is full of them."

"Why didn't you want to go to school in Manhattan?" I asked.

"My parents thought I needed to see new things," Paige said.

"I'm from a really small town," I said.

Paige turned down the stove heat. "A small town sounds nice. Manhattan is too busy. Too noisy. I wanted to come someplace a little quieter. My mom found Canterwood, we went on a tour, and that was that. Did you know that they even have cooking classes and gardening seminars here? They're my favorites!"

"Do you want to be a chef?"

Paige looked into the pot before looking at me. "Well, it's kind of my dream to be the next teen chef on The Food Network for Kids." Paige bit back a grin. "I went on a couple of auditions last year and didn't get it, but I'm going to try again during the next casting call."

I handed Paige a bowl for the soup. "I can help you practice—you'll snag the part next time."

"Deal." Paige and I laughed.

After downing Paige's grilled cheese and a bowl of soup, we each showered, brushed our teeth, and climbed into our beds to read. Paige chose *How to Survive Seventh Grade While Looking Fabulous* and I read *National Velvet* for the twenty-seventh time. It was one of my favorites.

At exactly ten thirty, just in case Livvie really was

patrolling the hall, I wiggled under my covers and opened my nightstand drawer. I pulled out my plastic retainer case, trying to hide it.

"What's that?" Paige asked.

"Retainer." I smiled sheepishly. "It's so embarrassing that I still wear one."

Paige rolled on her side and reached for her nightstand. She opened her drawer and pulled out a familiar red container.

"I wear mine every night," she said.

We put on our retainers and spent the first night in the dorm with my poster smiling over us.

4

PART OF A FAMILY

PAIGE AND I LEFT WINCHESTER AND HEADED for the cafeteria. Thank God Paige went with me. We got in the breakfast line and piled our plates high with eggs, cantaloupe, and toast. I scooted a couple of inches closer to Paige. I hoped she didn't think I was too clingy. There was no way I could do this alone. It looked as if everyone already had a table.

"Hey," Paige called to a table of girls across the room. They motioned her over. "Let's sit with them," she said to me. "They live in Winchester, too."

We walked across the room, passing tables of students. The cafeteria was a mix of long rectangular tables, small circular tables, and a few booths by the windows. High school and middle school students—some with jerseys and some with sketchpads—sat together. I noticed the students didn't seem to be as divided as they had been at my old school. At Union Middle School, I had eaten with the girls who had played team sports. None of my Briar Creek friends had gone to UMS; they had been in a different district or at local private schools. Even though I sat with the sporty girls at lunch, we weren't *really* friends. I didn't join them for slumber parties or go to the movies with them on weekends. We didn't even share makeup or fashion tips in between classes. All I ever thought about was riding, and all I ever wanted to do was spend time at the stable.

The girls at Briar Creek were nice, but they had a better bond with each other than with me, since they went to the same school. I was excited about my fresh start at Canterwood. Here, I had the chance to start over and make new friends.

I looked around me. Unlike the kids at UMS, the Canterwood kids sat in mixed social groups in the cafeteria. Band students mingled with the basketball team. Kids with paintbrushes poking out of their backpacks laughed with guys bouncing soccer balls on their knees. Much to my relief, there didn't seem to be a designated table for awkward newbies.

"Guys, this is Sasha," Paige said to them, motioning for me to slide into the plastic seat next to her. "She's my roommate in Winchester."

"Canterwood didn't scare you off yet?" an Asian girl next to me asked.

"No," I said, digging into my fruit. "But I haven't taken a science class yet, so we'll see." Paige introduced the girls.

"That's Annabella, Kristen, and Suichin." Annabella had a megawatt smile—and I vaguely remembered seeing Kristen around Winchester on move-in day. The girls acted as if I'd sat at their table every day.

"You'll love it here," Kristen said, finishing her orange juice. Her eyes caught on my horse charm. "Rider?"

"Yep, headed to the stables next," I said.

"Do you have a horse?" Kristen asked.

"His name is Charm," I said, grateful to talk about my favorite subject. "He's a chestnut Thoroughbred with a little bit of Belgian."

"Like a racehorse?" Annabella asked.

"He's a bit too heavy to race, but yeah," I laughed. "He'd love it that you thought of him as a racer."

"I race, too," Kristen said. "Suichin and I run track." The girls flashed matching gold pendants of a girl running pinned to their shirts.

"Hundred-meter dash and cross-country," Suichin bubbled.

Paige gulped down the last mouthful of cantaloupe. "I've got to swing by the student bookstore. Ready, Sasha?"

"See you later," I said, smiling as I got up from the table.

"Bye!" The girls called after us.

Paige led me outside.

"Do you know how to get to the stables from here?" she asked, shielding her eyes from the sun with her hand.

"I do. Thanks for everything!"

"I'll see you back at the dorm," Paige said with a smile. She pulled her sunglasses over her eyes and walked off.

I managed not to get lost and when I stepped up to Charm's stall, he let out a soft whicker and stuck his head over the door. "Hi, boy," I said, gently pushing him backward so I could get inside the stall. "You okay?" He stepped up to me, letting me hug him, and I squeezed his neck. "I missed you." Charm seemed to be begging for a treat. "Oh, I see how it is. The grooms must have spoiled you last night. It looks like they already brushed you. But let's get you sparkling."

I clipped Charm's green lead line to his halter, grabbed his tack box off the ledge by his door and led him out of the stall. There was an empty set of crossties a few stalls down. He stood still while I clipped the ropes to his halter. "Let's start with the currycomb, okay?" Charm seemed to blink in agreement. I grabbed the pink rubber currycomb and moved it in circles over his body. Barely any hair came off, thanks to Charm's daily groomings. I switched to the dandy brush and swept it over his neck, barrel, and flanks. "Like that, huh?" I asked Charm. He snorted and leaned into the brush strokes.

This was my third year riding Charm. The first horses I had ridden were gentle mares, barely willing to trot. I rode dozens of horses until I found Charm. Instead of naming the horses, their owners numbered them so they wouldn't get attached. High-spirited Charm had been starved for attention. Barely five years old, he was green and needed a firm rider.

I took Charm to Briar Creek two weeks later. Charm bucked me off for a few weeks, but then we settled into a rhythm. Now, he didn't run when I tried to catch him in the paddock and he didn't buck if his girth was fastened too tight. It took a few months of getting to know Charm before I decided to register him with the name Charm because he brought me luck from the first time I petted him.

I reached into the pink tack box and picked up the

hoof-pick. "Hoof," I commanded Charm as I ran my hand down his leg and squeezed about his fetlock. He shifted his weight and lifted his hoof. I bent over and picked dirt and sawdust out of it, rubbing my finger over his horseshoe. A little luck wouldn't hurt anyone—especially not me!

"Sasha Silver," a high-pitched voice called out.

I looked up and saw Heather, flanked by two other girls, making their way over to the crossties near our stall. I released Charm's hoof and stood, brushing the hair out of my eyes. The girls were identically dressed in tall black boots and breeches. Heather's lips curled into a glossy smile.

"Hi," I said. I finished Charm's hoof.

Heather and her friends squeezed together and sat on top of a tack trunk across from Charm's stall. One girl sported a chic, platinum blond bob and the other had coffee-brown hair that hung in gentle waves around her shoulders.

"How's your arm?" I asked Heather.

"Never better," she chirped.

"I just want to apologize again for what happened yesterday," I said. "Charm is usually so calm and easy to handle."

Charm snorted and bobbed his head.

"Have you met Julia and Alison?" Heather motioned to

the girls beside her. She said it like they were one person, Julia'n'Alison. "That's Julia." The girl with the bob smiled. "And Alison." Alison gave me a bright grin and tossed her hair.

"Hello," I said.

"So, anyway," Heather said. "We were thinking that since you're new and you test tomorrow, we'd love to give you a few tips before the team meeting. Not that you need them," she added hastily.

"That would be great!" I said. "Lately, I've been struggling with keeping Charm's head down. I thought about a standing martingale but—"

Alison shook her head and jumped in. "Mr. Conner doesn't allow seventh graders to use martingales. He thinks we'll overuse them."

"Oh," I said. "Then maybe you can give me a couple of pointers for testing."

"We'll meet you at eight tomorrow morning by your horse's stall," Heather said. They turned and headed down the aisle.

Charm was almost ready to get back to his stall.

"See, Charm?" I whispered, as he lifted his head and watched Heather and her friends walk away. "We're part of a family."

5

SORRY,
WRONG WAY

MY ALARM CLOCK BLARED AT SEVEN FIFTEEN, way too early for a Sunday.

I awoke drenched in sweat and gasping for a breath. In my nightmare, someone had set Charm loose and no one could find him. I called his name until I had no voice left. I was alone in the woods when I found Charm standing in the rocky bed of a creek, holding his left back leg inches off the ground. I had known it was broken right away.

I shuffled out of bed, and headed for the bathroom, eager to wash away the bad dream. I changed out of my pajamas and slipped into my shirt and breeches.

"I have a surprise for you," Paige said. I turned around and she handed me a plate of hot strawberry waffles and a glass of apple juice.

"How did you do that?" I asked, my mouth watering.

"Livvie," Paige said. "I told her about your test and she helped me make these in the dorm kitchen."

"Thank you so much!"

"You're welcome. You're going to do great, I know it!"

After I finished my waffles, I took a couple of quick yoga breaths—in-out, in-out, and swiped on a coat of my favorite lip gloss—supershiny peach—and headed for the stables.

"Charmy," I said. "Hi, boy!"

He grunted, sticking his head over the door, and eyed me. His ears pointed toward me and he checked my hands for treats. "Sorry, nothing now," I told him. "After our ride, I'll find you something."

Heather and her friends weren't here yet, so I grabbed a soft brush from Charm's tack box. Ten minutes went by and there was still no sign of Heather. Charm enjoyed the grooming, so I continued to brush him while we waited. At eight forty-five, I put down the brush. "Sorry, boy," I said. "Be back in a bit."

I closed the stall door and headed for the indoor arena. Heather obviously wasn't coming, so I went over to the meeting room. A neon green piece of paper on the door caught my attention. THE RIDING TEAM MEETING HAS BEEN MOVED TO THE OUTDOOR RING. I peered inside the indoor arena and saw chairs and a small table set up. It looked like the right place, but I'd follow the flier's instructions.

I walked through the entrance of the outdoor ring and saw that it was empty. The arena dirt had lines in it, like it had been smoothed overnight. There were no chairs or tables. Hmm. Did we stand for the meeting?

Nine o'clock rolled around and I was the only one standing in the outdoor ring. The unusually chilly morning air pricked my skin. I waited ten more minutes, pacing tracks in the arena. Surely I wasn't the only one who showed up today! There wasn't a place to sit, so I leaned against the fence. Five more minutes ticked by. I kicked the dirt. Where was everyone? Mr. Conner didn't look like the type of man to be late for anything.

Finally, I gave up and headed back to the barn. I walked slowly down the aisle, looking into a couple of stalls for Heather, Julia, or Alison. When I reached the indoor arena, I knew something was wrong. Where had the flier gone? My face flushed as I peered inside. Heather, Callie, Julia, and the rest of the team were gathered together, each of them seated on a folding chair. Did Heather forget about me? What about the sign on the door? Mr. Conner waved his hands as he spoke. I couldn't believe I was late for my first lesson!

Heather glanced toward the door as I entered and gave me a smile with a beauty queen wave.

Mr. Conner stopped talking. Everyone looked at me.

"Ms. Silver," Mr. Conner's voice boomed over the arena. "We start meetings promptly at nine."

"I saw a sign on the door that said—"

"No excuses, Ms. Silver. I expect you to be here on time. Prompt. Next time, you're on probation until I say otherwise. Clear?"

"Yes, sir," I said, my voice barely audible.

He motioned for me to take a seat and I headed for an empty chair in the back row.

When I passed Heather, she whispered, "Oops. Guess someone put the wrong directions on that flier."

Was this payback for the Charm incident? I'd apologized a million times! She had probably faked her arm injury, too. I folded my arms across my chest and stared straight ahead. About thirty riders filled the rows in front of me.

"Had you been on time," Mr. Conner started, with a glance in my direction. "You would have heard that this is one of the few times all of the students will be meeting together. From now on, you'll only be meeting with your specific class—whether it is beginner, intermediate, or advanced."

According to the riding team handbook, a student rarely reached advanced on his or her first test, so I'd be happy with beginner, but I was hoping, hoping, hoping for intermediate!

"Finally," Mr. Conner continued. "Remember that the Connecticut State Horse Show is a month away. I expect to see some hard practicing. To the three new students who are testing today: please prepare for your individual rides. The rest of you are free to go." Today, I'd use the F.A.B. technique that Kim taught me—focus, agility, balance. If Charm kept his head down, listened to my leg aids, and didn't get distracted by the new arena, maybe that would make up for Friday's disaster.

Heather got up and grinned. "Good luck, Sasha! We'll be in the skybox cheering you on!"

Just what I needed—an audience.

"You okay?" asked a voice behind me. It was Callie. I hadn't noticed before now how pretty she was. She had gorgeous mocha-latte skin, and soft, delicate features that projected a genuine sweetness. Her layered dark brown hair hung halfway down her back. "I saw you talking to Heather," she added. "Just . . . watch out for her. She plays dirty sometimes."

"She made me late to the meeting," I said.

"She pulled that trick last year," Callie said. "She, Julia, and Alison—the Trio—act like they own the place. Mr. Conner likes them because they're good riders, but he doesn't know how they really are."

"Mr. Conner thinks I'm a total idiot now. He'll be gunning for me the rest of the semester."

"He wants the team to succeed," Callie said. "If he sees you working hard, he won't pick on you."

"Any tips for impressing him on my ride?" I asked.

"He's a stickler for the basics. Keep the toes up, heels down and don't let your horse be in control. I've gotta go tack up and practice, but do you want to trail ride with me sometime?"

"That would be great," I said. "You can show me all of the good spots around here."

Callie nodded and headed off. I looked over at Mr. Conner. He gathered a massive stack of papers off the table and eyed me as I approached him.

"I don't have an excuse for being late," I said.

"Go tack up and be back here in fifteen minutes. Let's determine what level you're on."

"It won't happen again," I said. "I promise."

He put his stack of papers down, took a seat, and said, "We'll see."

6

PERFECT PAYBACK

"AGAIN!" MR. CONNER BARKED, HIS VOICE echoing in the large arena.

This was my chance to show him I belonged on this team. The Trio watched me from above. I chanted Callie's tips over and over in my head. Toes pointed up, heels pushed down. Toes pointed up, heels pushed down.

Charm was balanced beneath me. My fingers tensed on the reins whenever I saw Mr. Conner, but I tried to forget he was standing there.

I turned Charm in a circle and pointed him at the first descending oxer. Charm soared over the black-and-white rails, collected his canter in a few strides, and easily jumped two small verticals.

"Good boy," I whispered as we turned a corner and

headed for the plastic wall. If we could keep this up, we'd be in good shape. Charm rocketed off his back legs and propelled over the fake brick wall. His body pointed toward an in-and-out and he popped over both jumps. I kept my eyes focused between Charm's ears. Sensing my slight pressure on the reins, he slowed his fast pace into a rocking, smooth canter.

We headed for the final brush jump.

Charm tucked his legs neatly under his body and we soared over it. He eased into a trot and we circled around to Mr. Conner. Charm's heavy bursts of breath matched mine. We'd had a good ride.

"Nice job," Mr. Conner said when Charm halted in front of him. He motioned for me to dismount and, holding Charm's leather reins in my hands, I locked eyes with Mr. Conner.

"Thank you." My hands trembled as I took off my helmet. Charm shifted beside me. Mr. Conner looked down at his clipboard and scribbled a few notes. He flipped through his notebook, and then closed the cover and looked at me.

"For being the newest member on the team, you have a remarkably strong seat, a willing horse, and a nice jumping style. If you're committed to practicing every day and attending all meetings on time, I'm starting you off in the intermediate class. You'll attend lessons with Group A: Julia, Alison, Nicole, Heather, and Callie."

Intermediate! I could barely keep myself from dancing right there in the middle of the arena. "Thank you so much! Mr. Conner, you won't be disappointed."

"Make sure I'm not," he said and gave me a brief smile. He headed out of the arena to tell the next girl it was time to test. When he left, I turned to the skybox and grinned up at Heather, Julia, and Alison.

"See you at practice!" I called up to them.

Heather's face reddened. The other girls' eyes narrowed. Perfect payback.

I skipped all the way back to Charm's stall. We were officially part of the team! People would count on us and we had to do our best for the group.

Clipping him in crossties, I removed his sweaty tack and took him for a cooling walk. It was the perfect temperature for a Sunday stroll, windy but warm. "You were perfect," I told him. "You knew exactly what to do. You could have done the course without me."

I released Charm into his stall after our walk and headed out. I spotted a glass case on my way. I looked closer. Trophies, medals, and ribbons from the Canterwood Riding

Team filled every inch of space. A glossy wooden board with gold plaques hung beside the case. Each plaque had a name inscribed on it.

I stood in silence, staring at the glittering case. Charm and I could make it to the Rolex Kentucky—a pre-Olympic event—one day if we worked hard enough, I knew it. With one last glance at the case, I left the stable and dialed home from my cell.

"Intermediate!" I screamed into the phone when Dad answered. "Can you believe that?"

"Oh, Sasha! Wow!" Dad said. "I'm so proud of you!"

"I have a shot at the advanced team now," I said.

"Always looking ahead, huh?" Dad laughed. "Well, I'd hand the phone to Mom, but she just ran to the store. I won't spoil your news. I'll have her call you tonight and you can tell her then."

When I got back to the dorm, Paige wasn't there. My stomach rumbled. I was too hungry to wait for her to come back before I ate. What was I going to do every time Paige couldn't go with me? Starve?

I inhaled and exhaled, the way my yoga DVD had taught me—except for the whole breathing-into-your-center thing. What did that even mean, anyway?

A few minutes of yoga breathing and two coats of kiwi

lip gloss later, I found myself in line for a burger, fries, and soda.

I scanned the cafeteria. There was no one from Winchester or the riding team anywhere. Then I spotted an empty chair at a table near a big window where only one girl was sitting. When I got a few steps closer, I realized it was Livvie. Sitting with Livvie had to be better than sitting alone, right?

"Can I sit here?" I asked.

"Sure," she said, barely looking up from her wilted salad. "How are things so far?" she asked.

"Okay. I had my first riding team meeting today," I said. I thought about telling her how Heather tricked me, but decided it was safer not to.

Livvie smiled and offered me a carrot stick, which I took. "Don't worry," she soothed. "Work hard, and you'll be rewarded. Besides, everyone will do well this semester because we're all going to study, study, study! Right?"

Right.

When we finished our food, Livvie said, "Well, I better get back to the dorm. See you later!" She gave me a quick smile and got up from the table with her tray in hand.

I tossed my wadded napkin on my tray and headed for the exit. On my way out, I passed a group of guys when I noticed that one of them was the Zac Efron look-alike I'd seen outside my window my first day here!

I wanted to smile at him as I walked by, but I couldn't. A group of giggling girls walked by me and I followed behind them out of the cafeteria. The guy didn't notice me anyway. But maybe next time, I wouldn't be so tongue-tied.

After all—Union Sasha was shy around guys, but Canterwood Sasha didn't have to be.

7

BEGINNER'S LUCK

ON MONDAY MORNING, PAIGE AND I WERE OUT of the dorm by seven thirty. We both had our first class in the English building.

I looked at my schedule for the millionth time: English, biology, algebra, Spanish, history.

"Good luck," Paige said, before disappearing into a classroom down the hall.

"You, too," I whispered after her. I took one final deep yoga breath in, deep breath out, and walked into Room 307.

I scanned the room for an empty desk. A cluster of desks near the front of the room was empty, so I snagged one. *Whew.* If only I didn't have to change rooms.

I pulled a notebook and pen out of my backpack and

looked up at the mile-long list of textbooks taped to the dry erase board. Union Middle School hadn't been nearly as demanding as Canterwood. I'd known that before I'd even arrived on campus—the glossy, official-looking welcome packet I'd gotten with my acceptance letter was covered with the words "academic excellence," "high standards," "best," and "brightest." But sitting here now, staring at the list of books I'd be reading for my first Canterwood class, it felt much more real—and, honestly, much more intimidating. I'd never seen such a reading list! *To Kill a Mockingbird*, *Jane Eyre*, *The River Between Us*—the list went on and on.

"Hey, Sasha," Callie said, sliding into a seat next to me.

"Hey," I said, smiling. Thank God it was Callie and not Heather!

Callie set her binder down on her desk. It was bright yellow, covered with star and moon stickers. "Do you want to trail ride after class?" she asked.

"That'd be great." I knew Charm would be happy to get out of the stable.

"Good morning," Mr. Davidson said as he entered the room. "I'm Mr. Davidson and you'll be stuck with me this year for English. Go ahead and copy down the reading list and then we'll get started."

While everyone finished copying down the list, Mr. Davidson set up a CD player and opened a CD case. He selected a disc and placed it in the player.

"Since it's only our first day, let's read aloud and then analyze the first few pages of *A Tree Grows in Brooklyn* by Betty Smith. Who would like to read?"

Raise your hand, I told myself. Slowly, my hand went up.

Mr. Davidson smiled. "We have our first volunteer! Your name?" he asked.

"Sasha Silver." My voice was soft and wobbly. For a second, I wondered if Mr. Davidson had even heard me.

"Thank you, Sasha. Now, while you read, I'm going to play a bit of classical music in the background. Listen to the music and try to pace your reading with the rhythm of the music."

I looked around. My old UMS teachers had never done anything like that before.

"Okay," I said. I took a deep breath and started to read. "'Serene' was a word you could put to Brooklyn, New York . . . ,'" In the background, a light classical melody, with piano and violin, filled the room. The music was relaxing. A few sentences later, my breathing fell into rhythm with the music.

"Very nice, Sasha," Mr. Davidson said when I paused

at the end of the paragraph. "Did you hear how different Sasha sounded once she adjusted to the music?"

The class nodded.

"Who would like to read next?" Mr. Davidson asked.

A girl in the front row raised her hand and started to read the next paragraph. Callie slipped a folded pink Post-it into my lap. I glanced up to be sure Mr. Davidson wasn't looking; when he wasn't, I opened the note. *Good job.* ☺.

I grinned and wrote her back in purple ink. *Thanks!*

At the end of class, Callie and I loaded up our backpacks. "I've got biology with Ms. Peterson next," I said. "You?"

"Health with Mr. Henner. He's supposed to be tough." Callie wrinkled her nose. "Catch you later."

We split up in the hallway and I headed over to the science building. Instead of desks, the biology classroom had white lab tables, sinks, and microscopes. The air smelled like rubbing alcohol. I was the first one in the classroom, so I sat at a table in the center of the room. The rest of the class trickled in and I sighed with relief when the door closed and I didn't see Heather.

Then the door swung open, and Julia and Alison stepped inside, carrying matching pink bags. It was weird to see them without Heather. They both narrowed their eyes at me before taking a seat at the table across from me.

A short woman with dark hair swept back into a ballet bun entered the classroom and stood at the podium. "I'm Ms. Peterson and this is biology. Please get out a sheet of paper and a pen."

Uh-oh.

"I'm going to be asking you twenty-five questions. If you answer the majority of the questions correctly, it will be a good indication to me that you've done your summer reading. If not, you'll have lots of catching up to do."

Summer reading had been intense. I hadn't been able to make a dent in my fun book pile because I'd read school books all summer. I didn't even finish writing my name before Ms. Peterson began. "Question one: Name the six kingdoms."

My hand froze over my paper. I'd read about the kingdoms this summer but I had absolutely no *clue* how many of them there were! Pencils and pens scratched around me. *Plant,* I wrote. The girl next to me smiled at her paper and looked up at Ms. Peterson.

"Question two," Ms. Peterson said.

I sneaked a glance at Julia and Alison. They were looking

at Ms. Peterson, calmly waiting for the next question.

"Define *photosynthesis*," Ms. Peterson said.

I knew that one! I wrote down the definition, hoping that maybe the first question was the hardest. But as the questions continued, I knew I was in trouble.

"Please pass your quizzes forward," Ms. Peterson said, finally.

I handed my paper over to Julia; she held it and looked at my answers. She passed it over to Alison and they both snickered. Julia looked at me with one perfectly plucked eyebrow arched. *Loser*, she mouthed.

At least I knew the answer to one question: Least favorite class? Biology, hands down.

Back at the dorm, I dropped my book bag—which weighed about as much as a Falabella horse—and changed for my riding lesson.

I couldn't believe I'd failed my first quiz. I'd never failed anything in my life—not even a pop quiz!

Ms. Peterson had loaded us up with lots of homework. When I got back from riding lessons, I'd be studying the rest of the night.

My phone rang right as I was headed out the door.

"Hi, honey," Mom said. "How was your first day of

classes?" Her voice made me smile. It was babyish, but I still missed my parents.

"It was okay," I said. There was *no* way I was telling her about the quiz. "But I was just headed out for practice."

"Okay, we'll catch up later. And honey," she said in her best Mom voice, "just remember that it takes time to get used to things."

"Thanks, Mom," I said. I hadn't realized how much I missed her until I heard her voice.

After I hung up, I looked at myself in the mirror. I smoothed stress-relieving mint gloss over my lips and told my reflection that there was lots of time to make up for the quiz grade in bio.

At the stables, I unlatched Charm's stall door.

Callie was crouched behind Charm in the corner by his blue water bucket. She stood and held a finger up to her lips in a "shhh" motion.

When I stepped inside, she pulled the stall door shut behind me.

"What's going on?" I asked.

"You have to keep an eye on your tack," she whispered. Her dark hair was pulled into a low ponytail and she looked like she had been scrubbing tack for hours.

Yellow saddle soap caked on her hands and wrists and a few streaks of soap were on her face.

"My saddle and bridle?" I asked. "Why?"

"Heather has been lurking around the tack room all day. I'd watch your stuff. She's in an especially nasty mood."

"Did Heather do something to your tack?" I asked.

Callie grinned sheepishly. "No, mine was just dirty. But it seems like she's out for you."

"I don't get it," I said. "What's her problem?"

Callie stepped away from me and peered over Charm's stall door, as though making sure Heather wasn't within earshot.

"I'll tell you about it on the trail ride. We're still on for later, right?"

"Right after practice."

Callie tiptoed out of the stall and headed to tack up her horse.

I'd thought the flier trick would have been payback enough from Heather. I left Charm and went to the tack room to get his gear.

The tack room's wooden door was ajar—voices came from inside.

"She can't help where Mr. Conner placed her," said

a voice that sounded like Julia's. "What can we do about it?"

"She's better than I thought." Another voice—sour and forceful. Heather. "We can't let her take a spot on the advanced level. Only five students from our grade can have a spot on the advanced team. And I *have* to be one of them."

"Of course you'll get a spot, Heather," Alison said. "She's in over her head. She totally failed the bio quiz today, too. Julia and I saw. This is *Canterwood*; she'll be packing for Hicksville by the end of the month."

"Of course she will," Heather agreed. "But I'm not taking any chances. We deserve those seats, not her."

I couldn't stand there and listen to this anymore. I pushed open the door. Julia and Alison stared at me from the corner of the room and didn't say a word. But Heather took one step toward me and crossed her long, slender arms over her chest.

"Sasha," Heather purred. "Have you been *spying* on us?"

"No," I said, my cheeks burning. "Look, Heather, I—"

"Save it, Silver," Heather spat. "You think you're so great just because you made the intermediate team?"

Julia and Alison smiled behind Heather.

"Beginner's luck," Julia said.

Heather laughed. "Seriously?" she continued, jutting her hip to one side. "You're wasting your time. If I were you, I wouldn't even bother showing up for practice."

One by one, each member of the Trio brushed past me and sauntered out the door.

Alone with the saddles, bridles and saddle pads, I checked every piece of my gear. Nothing seemed to have been moved. My saddle girth was in place, the strap on my helmet wasn't loose and Charm's bridle was untouched.

Charm stood quietly as I rubbed his shoulder and tacked him up. I led him to our first practice session, forcing myself to walk with my chin up. Inside the ring, Callie was warming up. Charm watched, with ears pricked forward, and looked at the new horse. On my tiptoes, I scratched between his ears, and Charm lowered his head so I didn't have to stretch.

"Charm looks good," Nicole said, riding up beside me. "He's a Thoroughbred mix, right?"

Charm flexed his neck, as though from her compliment. He liked people to know about his Thoroughbred blood. "Yeah," I said. "What's yours?" I hopped into the saddle and looked at Nicole.

"Hanoverian," she said

Mr. Conner entered the arena and we started to line up

the horses in the center. Nicole leaned over and whispered, "Welcome to the team." I shot her a grin and quickly turned my attention to Mr. Conner. I could feel Heather's eyes on me from across the arena, but I didn't lose focus during the entire hour-and-a-half session. Not once.

8

TRAIL RIDING AND DAYDREAMING

"THIS IS THE BEST PART OF THE TRAIL," CALLIE said, looking over the hill.

Charm slowed and Callie pulled her gelding, Black Jack, next to me. Black Jack was a Morab—a black Arabian and Morgan mix.

The rolling Connecticut hills boasted a forest with millions of green leaves tinged with red and gold, hinting that autumn was near.

This part of the trail reminded me of the woods behind Briar Creek where Charm and I had gone every week. Charm loved exploring the dirt paths that snaked around Kim's property. If we went out early in the morning and waited by one of the field's edges, we sometimes found a herd of deer. The deer seemed to like Charm; if I sat still, they'd stare at him for minutes.

Callie turned Black Jack as he picked his way down a rocky path littered with broken twigs and pinecones.

"How long have you been riding at Canterwood?" I asked.

Callie steadied Jack. "Since I started middle school in sixth grade. But if Canterwood would have had an elementary school, I would have so been here. I rode for the New England Saddle Club before this."

"I've heard of them. Did you ever do an event in Worthington?" I asked.

"Two years ago." Callie said. "The Sommersby Show. It was really exciting! I won first in dressage and second in cross-country and show jumping."

"I was in the audience!" I said, stopping Charm from taking a bite of leaf.

I remembered that show well—it was the first time Kim had broached the idea of me applying to Canterwood. All of the Canterwood riders had worn matching green and gold jackets. And beside the trailers, Canterwood's hunter green tents were staked into the ground. They even had catered food inside their tents. It had all seemed so glamorous and fancy. After that, I couldn't stop thinking about Canterwood.

"Heather was there too, I think, but that was before I knew her." Black Jack flicked his ears backward at the sound of Callie's voice.

"She wants to make the advanced team more than anything," I said.

Callie nodded. "We all do."

"How does the advanced riding team work, exactly?" I asked.

"Well, each year riders in grades seven and up at the intermediate level are allowed to try out for the advanced team," Callie said. "Only five riders from each grade make it. Sometimes no one makes it."

"Are you excited to try out?" I asked.

"Definitely," Callie said.

"So, do you think Heather's a shoo-in for the team?" When I said Heather's name, I swear, Charm shivered and shook his head.

"She's pretty good," Callie said. "But Julia, Alison, and a bunch of other seventh-grade intermediate riders are good, too."

"What about you? You're a great rider!" I said.

Callie tugged on Black Jack's reins to stop him from taking a bite of grass. "Riding is important. But

Mr. Conner wants riders with the total package—team skills, solid riding and good grades."

"Good grades? Does the advanced team have a minimum GPA?" My stomach tightened when I thought about my biology quiz.

"Both the advanced team and the Youth Equestrian National Team both require a B average."

"I didn't know that," I said. The YENT was like a Junior Olympic–caliber team for riders in eighth grade and high school. If Charm and I made that team, we had a shot at the Olympics in college.

My mind drifted back to Heather. It reminded me of the fight Heather and her dad had on campus that first day. "How are Heather's grades?" I asked.

Callie seemed to consider the question. "Heather's smart—she just doesn't work hard at anything but riding. Her parents expect a lot of her. They want her to go Ivy. Plus, her brother's a genius. I heard he was the youngest kid ever to be accepted into Stanford Law."

"Who worries about college in seventh grade?" I asked.

Callie tucked a strand of chocolate-colored hair behind her ear. "Everyone at Canterwood."

"It was really different where I used to go to school," I said.

"There's pressure on everyone to get good grades and pick the right extracurriculars and electives for college," Callie continued. "Straight As aren't enough."

"I hadn't even thought about that," I admitted. "Just thinking about whether or not I have a shot at the advanced team has been enough stress for me!"

"If you work hard, you could make it." Callie pulled Black Jack next to Charm as the trail widened. "I've seen your show jumping during practice. You're definitely one of the best stadium jumpers here."

I smiled. There hadn't been many compliments on my riding since I'd been here. "Thanks! It's my favorite eventing class. Charm loves it, too."

Now Charm and I had something to shoot for—the best stadium jumpers at Canterwood. Blue ribbons filled my head—I could almost hear the crowd's cheers. Scouts for the YENT would mob us with offers to come join them. Charm seemed to sense my daydream and tugged the reins to get me back to reality.

We continued our way down the dirt path, taking in the quiet. I thought about what Callie had said. Callie was one of the best riders I'd ever met. If *she* thought I was good, maybe I really did have a shot.

F IS FOR FRIDAY

I'd survived my first week of classes. English was still my favorite and algebra wasn't too hard either.

Ms. Peterson had passed back our quizzes on Tuesday. My grade—a sixty. As in, F. I'd pretty much assumed I'd failed the quiz already, but it didn't stop me from nearly having a heart attack when I saw the letter on top of my paper. Thankfully, Ms. Peterson told us that quiz wouldn't count, but to be prepared for a quiz on Monday.

Thank God.

I was *never* going to get an F again. I planned to spend double the amount of time studying biology from now on.

By Wednesday, I no longer felt nervous about going

to the cafeteria by myself, and I was even too busy to feel homesick.

Paige caught up with me in the hallway after math. "Going back to the dorm?" she asked.

"I've got to check in with the guidance counselor and pick an elective class," I told her.

"Have fun," Paige said. "There are some good ones this semester."

When I got to Ms. Utz's office, I signed in with the secretary and took a seat. A guy slid into the chair next to me.

"You here for Utz?" he asked.

For a second, I almost wasn't sure he was talking to me. "Yeah, I have to pick an elective," I said, turning toward him.

Oh. My. God.

It was the Zac Efron cutie! Up close, he was even hotter. He had a tiny freckle on his chin and a braided leather bracelet on his right wrist.

He smiled, showing gorgeous teeth, and leaned a little closer. He could do whitening commercials, seriously. "Yeah, I already did my schedule, but she signed me up for honors algebra. Twice."

"Yikes, I hope she doesn't do that to me!" Speaking

wasn't easy since all I could focus on was his gorgeous dark hair.

"I'm Jacob, by the way," he said.

"I'm Silver. Sasha. Sasha Silver." Ugh.

Jacob grinned. "You're new, right?"

"Yeah," I said. Omigod! He'd noticed me? He knew that I was new? He'd noticed me enough to know that I was new?!

"Some words of advice," Jacob said, leaning in and flicking his blue-green eyes toward the door. (*Swoon*). "Just watch Utz. She's kind of scary. Rumor is, she wrestles on the weekends."

I laughed. Out of the corner of my eye, a large woman in hunter green clogs appeared in the doorway. "Sasha Silver?" she called.

Jacob gave me a smile before I—reluctantly—followed Ms. Utz into her office. A large, gold championship ring glittered on her finger. I wondered if Jacob was right about the wrestling.

"Sit," she boomed, her voice reverberating off the walls in the tiny office. "So, how was your first week of classes at Canterwood?" She gave me a crooked smile and showed huge, square teeth.

"It was great," I said.

"Good," Ms. Utz said. "Now, you've already got riding as an extracurricular. That's enough for your first year. But you still need to pick an elective class. Here are your options." She slid a piece of paper across the table to me.

I scanned the page. Web design, environmental science, art history, music appreciation, film.

"Film sounds perfect," I said. "I love movies!"

"Film starts next Friday with Mr. Ramirez," Ms. Utz said. "You're all set!"

I grabbed my papers and pulled out my chair.

"Have a good semester," Ms. Utz called after me.

"Thank you," I said back.

Outside her office, Jacob's chair was empty. I looked at my watch and gasped. I was five minutes late to my riding lesson!

When I pulled Charm into the outdoor arena, Mr. Conner held up a hand to stop Julia, Alison, Nicole, Heather, and Callie, who were circling him on horseback at a trot.

"Everyone, please dismount," Mr. Conner said, tapping his toe in the dirt.

"Mr. Conner, I'm so sorry," I said, pulling Charm behind me as we jogged over to him.

Mr. Conner crossed his arms. "I'm guessing no one told you about our new late policy."

I shook my head.

"If a rider is late to a lesson, then the entire rest of the class must finish the remainder of the lesson from the ground, not the saddle."

There was no way I could keep up with Charm. He had Thoroughbred blood!

"Please get behind Heather," Mr. Conner said.

Great. Now she was going to hate me even more!

Charm and I halted a few steps behind Aristocrat. "Nice job, Silver," she hissed.

"Sorry," I mouthed.

Up ahead, Julia and Alison's faces were mashed into pouts. At least Callie and Nicole gave me sympathetic looks.

"Trot, please," Mr. Conner called out, resuming the lesson.

"C'mon, Charm," I said, giving him a gentle tug on the reins. I started jogging and Charm trotted beside me, careful not to bump me as we circled the arena. After our third circle, my forehead was dotted with sweat and the heels of my boots seemed to sink further into the ground.

"Walk," Mr. Conner called. Two horses in front of me, Alison's Arabian pulled her forward. Sunstruck didn't want to slow down. She whispered to him and got him to a walk.

"Bring your horses to the center," Mr. Conner said.

Julia sighed loudly and led Trix beside Charm. The mare was smaller than Charm, but she kept up. "You just *had* to be late," she grumbled.

"Sorry," I said, for what felt like the hundredth time.

Julia glared at me. "Don't do it again."

Mr. Conner tapped his crop against his boot. "Let's end the lesson with bending exercises." He motioned to Mike, one of the grooms, who watched from the fence. Mike hurried into the arena, carrying our halters and lead lines.

"Put on the halters, loosen your girths, and we'll get started," Mr. Conner said. Each of us slipped off our horses' bridles and replaced them with a halter. Mike took our bridles and left the arena.

"Okay," Mr. Conner continued. "We want the horses to be supple on both sides."

"What do you mean?" Callie asked.

"Like people, most horses have a stronger side. It's like being right- or left-handed. We want to teach them to be strong on both. Now, grab the lead line about six inches under the chin."

We all did. Charm squeezed his eyes shut. The poor guy was sleepy!

"Since we're just loosening them up, we're only going to do this for five seconds on each side," Mr. Conner said. "I'm going to hand each of you the end of your horse's tail and you're going to hold the lead line *and* the tail. Don't let go of either. The pressure on the tail and neck will make your horse bend and circle. Take small steps and let them circle for a few seconds and then release the tail."

Mr. Conner stepped up to Nicole and nodded at her gelding, Wishful Thinking. "Let me show you," he said. Nicole handed him the lead line and Mr. Conner took a handful of Wish's tail and kept a grip on the lead line. Wish started to bend and Mr. Conner let him circle twice before letting him go. "Now that was his good side," Mr. Conner said. "Watch as we circle to the right."

Wish took several clumsy steps in the right direction and moved slower than he had to the left. Mr. Conner released him and handed him back to Nicole.

"We'll go down the line," Mr. Conner said. "I'll help each of you."

I was last in line and when Mr. Conner got to me, Charm was almost snoring.

Mr. Conner eased Charm's tail into my hand and Charm took a step to the side.

"Good," Mr. Conner said. "A little more."

"You can do it, boy," I whispered to Charm. He took a few more steps and then I let go of his tail. Mr. Conner handed it to me again from the other side and Charm took a hesitant step. "It's okay," I said. "C'mon." Charm bent to the pressure on his neck and turned.

"All right, good!" Mr. Conner said. "Charm's almost smooth on both sides. Nice job, everyone."

I rubbed Charm's chin. "Hear that, boy? Smooth on both sides."

He nudged me and closed his eyes. "All right," I said, "let's go take a nap."

10

WHO'S AFRAID OF
A LITTLE FRIENDLY
COMPETITION?

IT WAS A WARM THURSDAY AFTERNOON AND Mr. Conner was supervising our outdoor jumping. Charm and I were finally fitting in after almost two weeks at Canterwood. It was nonstop practice for the Connecticut State Horse Show on the first weekend of October. Since testing for the advanced team wasn't until mid-November, the show was my first priority.

Charm cantered in a wide circle as we headed toward the hogsback jump. The three-foot fence loomed in front of us. Heather cantered alongside me on Aristocrat. She edged Aristocrat over and our boots almost brushed together. With a snort, Charm weaved over to the left.

"What are you doing?" I glared at her while trying to keep Charm in a straight line.

"Practicing," Heather called back. She smirked, veering Aristocrat closer. "You do know what practice is, don't you?" Her voice was barely audible over the quick thud of hoofbeats. I ignored Heather and edged closer. She watched me with narrowed eyes, trying to see if I would back out or force her off the fence. The jump looked as if it grew taller with each step Charm took. Seconds before Charm reached the jump, I sat deep in the saddle and pulled back on the reins. He tossed his head and snorted.

"We'll get the next one," I soothed, rubbing his taut neck.

Heather and Aristocrat surged past us and cleared the jump. She swung him around in a sharp circle to face us. A cloud of dust poofed under his hooves.

"What was that?" I asked, growing more and more furious with each failed attempt at a yoga breath.

"I took my jump," Heather said, keeping Aristocrat's head high in the air.

Charm pawed the ground. "Charm could have been hurt. You could have hit us!"

"Please." Heather rolled her eyes. "I was in control. Nothing happened."

"But it could have." Charm tensed under me.

"I didn't see you pull up immediately and—" Heather

closed her mouth when Mr. Conner strode between us. Goosebumps covered my arm. Heather had one thing right—I should have stopped Charm the second she started the game of chicken.

Mr. Conner's hands were balled into fists. He looked at me and then back at Heather. "What was that?" His face was bright red. "Someone explain this to me, now."

Callie was working on Jack's extension in the next ring, but when she heard Mr. Conner, she turned and gave me a sympathetic look.

Heather dropped the reins and crossed her arms. "Mr. Conner, we accidentally bumped together," she said.

"How big a fool do you think I am?"

"It really was an accident," I said. Mr. Conner turned away from me to face Heather. She gave him her trademark what-I'm-an-angel smile.

"And you?" he asked.

"Well, I didn't want to say anything before, but Sasha really is a dangerous rider. I was heading for the jump, Mr. Conner, and Sasha deliberately rammed into me. She could have injured us."

I couldn't believe it! My mouth dropped open. Mr. Conner turned to me. When his back was to Heather, she caught my eye and smirked.

"Mr. Conner," I said. "It wasn't like that at all."

"Then tell me what it was like," he said. His stern voice made me shiver in my warm jacket.

"Heather ran into us when we headed for the jump." With every word I spoke, I could feel Heather's eyes burning into me. "But I should have pulled up sooner."

Mr. Conner sighed. "Get your story straight, girls. I don't know who started this little rivalry and frankly, I don't care. You both could have been injured. Charm and Aristocrat could have torn a ligament or worse— broken a leg. Cool down your horses and put them away. Once they're back in their stalls, I want you both in my office."

I kicked Charm into a trot and headed for his stall. We walked around for ten minutes before I brushed him and put him away. Charm stepped into his stall and took a drink. I dragged my feet down the aisle, and with one last glance at Charm, who was still drinking, shuffled to Mr. Conner's office.

Heather stood outside his door. "You know he'll take my word over yours," she whispered.

Maybe Heather was right. I'd done nothing but mess up in front of Mr. Conner. But no matter what she said, I would never have intentionally put Charm or Aristocrat in danger.

"Are you gonna knock on the door or what?" Heather asked.

"Sure, if you can't even knock on a door without help, I'll do it for you," I said, surprising myself with my own courage.

I rapped at the door, but I could feel Heather's eyes growing wide beside me.

"Come in," Mr. Conner said.

Heather pushed in front of me and took the only chair. I stood beside her and clenched my hands.

"It appears that we have a serious safety issue," Mr. Conner started. "You both displayed very questionable behavior out there today." Mr. Conner shook his head. "I don't care how long you've been here, whether you're new or not. I'm disappointed in both of you."

"Sasha has been deliberately provoking me," Heather said. "She's trying to secure her spot on the advanced team by baiting me. I'm not sure if I can ride with her anymore."

"Being on a team, Ms. Fox, means being part of the group." Mr. Conner's tone was firm. He rubbed his hand across his chin and his large gold wristwatch flashed in the sunlight streaming inside his office window. "If you want to be part of the Canterwood riding team, you will do just that—be a part of the team. Is that going to be a problem?"

Heather sunk low in her seat. "No, sir, that's not a problem."

"This won't happen again," I offered.

"Good. And to ensure that it *doesn't*, you two are going to be spending more time together. Saturday morning. Seven o'clock. You will both be here, mucking stalls." He looked back down at his desk and picked up an envelope. "And remember that all of this will be taken into account when I decide who gets a seat on the advanced team. You're excused."

Heather pushed her chair back and tiptoed out the door.

I raced to Charm's stall, leaving her behind.

I barely made it inside the stall before the tears started. "I'm so sorry, Charm," I whispered to him. He looked at me, his soft eyelashes fluttering, and nudged me with his velvety muzzle. "You could have gotten hurt today. And it would have been all my fault. We should have backed off the second Heather headed for the jump." I wrapped my arms around Charm's strong neck and rested my head against him. He leaned into me and, in his own way, hugged me back.

"Sasha?" Callie's head poked over the stall door. She

came into the stall and stroked Charm's neck. "Heather headed right for you," she assured me. "All you could do was pull him up."

I shook my head. "I shouldn't have let him go that far. Something just came over me and I didn't want to let her take the fence."

"But you stopped," Callie said. "Heather didn't. It wasn't your fault."

"Charm is okay and that's all that matters," I conceded, wiping tears away with the back of my hand.

"C'mon, let's go," Callie said. "I'll buy you a smoothie."

I gave Charm one last good-bye pat and secured the door. Callie and I linked arms and headed away from the stables.

After the afternoon I'd had, I was glad to have a friend like Callie to leave with. No matter what the Trio said to me, I had Charm, Callie, and Paige to remind me why I came to Canterwood in the first place. Anyway, I wasn't about to let anyone bully me into leaving.

11

HE SMELLED
MY LIP GLOSS

THE CANTERWOOD MEDIA CENTER WAS JUST across campus from Winchester. I'd never been there before, but Paige told me it had a massive movie theater, a TV lounge, computers, and video games.

I was going to my first film class—we were supposed to meet in the theater, listen to a brief lecture from the teacher, and watch a movie.

Inside the brightly lit theater, three rows of seats were roped off and a paper sign had been posted that read "seventh-grade film class—please sit in your assigned seat." I scanned the rows until I spotted a piece of paper with my name taped to the back of a chair. Sinking into the deeply cushioned red chair, I opened my purple notebook and wrote *film class*. It looked like a small class, only about fifteen seats had papers on them. A couple of girls found their seats in front of me.

"Excuse me," one of my classmates said as he stepped in front of me and took a seat on my left.

I looked out of the corner of my eye, and when I saw who was sitting there, I could have *died*!

Jacob.

When he pulled his notebook out of his bag, our arms almost touched and I looked away from him. Okay, I could do this. Just ignore the pounding heart and be cool. But I knew I wouldn't be able to be cool. Those eyes, that gorgeous hair—he even *smelled* good— like peppermint. This called for a lip gloss action plan! Digging into my jacket pocket for a tube, I found one of my favorites—s'mores. I applied a thick coat.

Jacob looked at me. "Hey, you're the new girl from Utz's office—Sasha, right?"

O.M.G.

I nodded and gave him what I hoped was a cute smile.

He shifted in his seat. "What's that smell?" he asked.

Oh *no*. Did I smell like horse? Or worse . . . manure? I glanced to the other side and took a quick whiff of my shirt. Secret Vanilla with a hint of caramel body wash. Maybe I didn't smell the horse scent because I was too used to it! Too many years at the stable. Too many years of muck. And horses. And hay. Dear God, I was immune! I could smack myself for not taking Paige's offer to make me cinnamon sachets for my sock drawer.

"What smell?" I asked, my cheeks pink.

He sniffed the air. "It's chocolate. I can't figure out where it's coming from."

Phew! Chocolate definitely wasn't horsey. I jammed my hand into my jean pocket and produced the lip gloss. "It's this," I explained, holding it up.

He peered at the label with gray green eyes and laughed. "It's making me hungry. You don't have a cheeseburger-scented one, do you?"

"Nope, sorry." I said, shaking my head. New mission: find cheeseburger-scented lip gloss. I'd have to hit Sephora.com the second I got back to the dorm.

I hadn't even noticed that people had filled the seats around us.

A gangly man with a pale face stood in front of the class. He was dorky in a Peter Parker pre-spider-bite sort of way. He took a deep bow. "I'm Mr. Ramirez," he said. "Welcome to your first film class. In this class, I'll be taking you on a journey through the world of film. We'll be covering classics like *E.T.*, cartoon blockbusters like *Toy Story,* and love stories such as *Titanic.*"

The theater was quiet. Mr. Ramirez continued. "You've probably heard this is an easy class." Several girls in front of me nodded. "Well, that's not *exactly* true. You'll write papers, learn film terminology, and memorize many film quotes."

The guy on my right shifted over and put his arm on the armrest.

"Let's start with a little comedy to lighten the mood," Mr. Ramirez said. "We'll be screening the 1959 classic, *Some Like it Hot,* with Marilyn Monroe." He turned down the lights.

"I've seen this movie a couple of times," Jacob whispered. Hopefully, he couldn't hear my pounding heart. I didn't have the nerves for this boy thing!

The enormous movie screen crackled as the film started. Jacob and I sat in silence for a few minutes, but soon we were laughing at the movie at all the same parts. He caught my eye a couple of times and my earlier embarrassment started to fade. I forgot about my English paper due next week and the fact that Charm and I had knocked a rail during practice yesterday. All too soon, the movie ended. The lights came on, with an annoyingly bright glare, and Jacob shot me a smile.

Mr. Ramirez stood in front of the screen and clapped his hands. "We have so much time, and so little to do! Strike that, reverse it."

"*Willy Wonka and the Chocolate Factory*!" Jacob called out.

"Correct, sir! And you are?" Mr. Ramirez asked.

"Jacob Schwartz."

Mr. Ramirez stepped into the row in front of us and sat on the back of a chair. "What did you think of the film, Jacob?"

Jacob didn't hesitate. "I think that any guy who wants to understand girls should watch the film." His comment sent Mr. Ramirez and the entire class into laughter.

"Anyone else?"

I raised my hand and he nodded to me.

"The movie seemed like it may have been ahead of its time," I said.

"Good, good. Your name, please?" Mr. Ramirez asked, a smile on his face as he rubbed his clean-shaven chin with his hand.

"Sasha Silver."

"That was a good observation, Sasha. So, if the movie was ahead of its time, why do you think the studio took a risk on it?"

"Probably because it's so funny. People come to the movies to escape."

"That's very good. Quite true." Mr. Ramirez moved off to another row.

After a few more questions, he brought up the dreaded topic of homework.

"Each of you will need to choose a film and write a three-page paper about it. The topic is up to you. You may use a film from the library or from your own collection. To ensure you read the syllabus, I'm not going to tell you the paper's due date."

The rest of the class began packing up their books. I tried to think of something else to say to Jacob. "Good movie," I said finally.

L.A.M.E.

"Yeah, it was." He grinned and, with that, headed out of the theater, disappearing into the crowd.

"He did what?" Paige asked.

"He smelled my lip gloss." I crashed onto my bed with a sigh. "Paige, we've been talking about this for twenty minutes! There's not much left to tell."

She ignored me and flopped onto my bed. "How many times have you seen him? He definitely likes you."

Rolling my eyes, I got up off the bed and switched on my laptop. "I don't know. And anyway, all he said when we left was 'see you around.'"

"That could mean anything. Like, 'maybe I'll see you around' or 'see you for sure at the next class.' What a typical guy. Totally murky response."

"I'm shopping for lip gloss. How about bubble gum?" I waved an arm at Paige. Mom and Dad had given me a credit card for emergencies—this definitely counted!

Paige wrinkled her nose. "Sasha, you've got to get scents *he* would like. Bubble gum is a *girl* smell." She stared at my computer screen and scrolled through the massive lip gloss collection.

"Is there anyone at Canterwood you like?" I asked her.

"I do like someone at home," she confessed. "Do you remember that picture I showed you of me dancing?"

I nodded, remembering the picture—Paige arm in arm with her tall, gorgeous dance partner.

She smiled. "His name is Derek. But my mom doesn't approve. She thinks he's a good dance partner, but he's the instructor's son. He sends me e-mails sometimes." Paige pointed to the screen. "What about this one?"

"Tangerine? Fruit is better than bubble gum?"

"It's very aromatic—guys have a nose for citrus scents,"

Paige explained. "And here's one—cinnamon. And mint!"

We scanned the screen and kept an eye out for the elusive and nonexistent cheeseburger flavor.

"How about vanilla bean?" I asked, adding it to the cart. I'd be going home next Friday while the teachers had their staff development day. Hopefully, Mom and Dad wouldn't see their credit card bill before then.

12

I DON'T WANT YOUR
STUPID SWEATSHIRT

"IF YOU GET MANURE NEAR MY FOOT AGAIN, I'm going to scream!" Heather threatened.

After three hours of this, on a Saturday no less, it was a miracle that her squealing hadn't deafened me by now. Her hair was pulled into a flawless ponytail, not a single glossy tendril daring to escape. My hair, on the other hand, was matted with sweat. I wiped my filthy hands on ancient gray sweatpants that sagged in the butt and had holes in the knees.

The scent of manure filled the stall. Breathing through my mouth, I stuck my pitchfork in the sawdust and spread it around the stall. At least next weekend, I'd be home for three days. Not seeing Heather for seventy-two hours sounded *so* good.

Mike led Charm and Aristocrat side by side down the aisle. The horses eyed each other warily. They pulled on the lead lines, tugging Mike forward to the turnout pasture. I watched out the window as Mike put Charm in one paddock and Aristocrat in another. They regarded each other over the dark wooden fence line and Aristocrat let out a challenging neigh. Great, now Charm and Aristocrat were fighting. Dark gray thunderclouds gathered in the distance. Mike would probably bring the horses back inside soon.

My arms, back, and neck burned. My boots were filled with sawdust. Dirt stuck under my fingernails and sawdust clumped in my hair.

Heather's cell phone rang from her pocket—some typical pop song I'd heard a thousand times over the summer. Surprise, surprise. She threw her pitchfork down and jammed her hand into her tiny pocket.

"We're supposed to be working," I reminded her.

She waved her hand at me dismissively and walked outside the stall to talk, but her voice carried enough for me to hear.

"Dad, it's my math teacher, Ms. Utz. She hates me! She's going to fail me." She paused and listened. I could hear gravel crunch beneath her feet as she paced back and forth. "Okay, okay. Bye."

For a second, I almost felt bad for her. It sounded like her dad never stopped pressuring her. No wonder she was so cranky all the time.

Heather entered the stall. She avoided my eyes and started shoveling damp sawdust out of the stall. Reason told me to keep my big mouth shut, but my lips didn't listen. "You okay?" I asked.

Heather glared at me. "Like you care," she said.

"Just asking," I said.

"Why did you even come here?" Heather jabbed the pitchfork in the sawdust and crossed her arms over her chest. "*You* don't have a mother who was almost an Olympic equestrian. *You* haven't been bred for Canterwood since you were four."

"I placed in every show in my district," I said. "And I was first at Briar Creek."

"*Briar Creek*?" Heather laughed. "You can't be serious. Oh God, you are. You think showing well for a third-rate stable on the bottom tier makes you a good rider? Silver, the advanced level at Briar Creek, is like beginner here. I drove past that little hole-in-the-wall on my way to the West Hartford spring show last year."

My fingers gripped the wooden pitchfork handle and my heart thudded.

"Briar Creek may not have a big reputation, but the riders are good," I said.

Heather rolled her eyes. "You may have won all of the shows at your level, but you haven't ridden at ours. All of our riders are great. Not *good*."

All traces of sympathy I had for Heather while she was on the phone with her dad were gone now. "What did I ever do to you, Heather?" I asked, looking right at her. "What is your *problem*?"

Heather sighed like she was bored of me, but I could tell she wasn't expecting me to talk back to her. "The only reason Mr. Conner put you in intermediate, and not beginner, is so you'd fail faster and quit," she said. "Better to realize now that you don't have what it takes than waste your time trying to move up the ranks later."

I could feel my face getting warm. It took all of my restraint not to throw manure on her. I had to get out of here. Heather could muck by herself.

I left the stall to check on Charm. Charm and Aristocrat, in opposite ends of their pastures, ignored each other and snipped the grass with their teeth. My reflection in the mirror showed my hair sticking out in tangles and a tiny zit forming on my forehead. Paige had me on a new beauty regimen—nightly facials and something with a weird, unpronounceable acid—to impress Jacob. But so far, all I'd done was break out.

Thunder rumbled overhead. Mike dashed by me with lead lines flapping in his hands. "I'll get Charm!" I yelled after him as we raced outside. Charm jerked his head up from the grass when he spotted me running toward his pasture.

"Thanks, Sasha," Mike said, tossing me his extra lead line. He headed for Aristocrat's pasture.

Charm trotted over to the gate and waited for me to reach him. "Let's go before you get wet," I said to him. One pasture over, Mike caught Aristocrat and led him toward the stables. Charm, not wanting to be the last one inside, stretched out into a trot.

By the time I got back, Mr. Conner had arrived.

"Stalls look good," he said, surveying our work. "Consider your sentence served. You may go now—unless you want to continue."

"No, we're good," I said.

Mr. Conner smiled and headed back to his office.

"I'll start rinsing the buckets, if you put away the pitchforks," I said to Heather.

"Do it, instead of talking about it." She stalked off, dragging the pitchforks behind her.

I tossed the dirty rubber bucket inside the concrete wash stall, squirted a bit of cleanser into the bucket, and turned the hose on full blast. The green hose that snaked around the stall flooded the bucket with cold water. Suddenly, the water stopped. I shook the hose, but still—nothing. When I turned the corner, I found a kink in the hose. I crouched down, my tired fingers fumbling with the kink. Outside, rain began to fall and pounded the roof, almost drowning out the sound of the hose.

Just as I unkinked the hose, a scream rose from the stall. "Turn it off! Turn it off!"

I twisted off the valve and ran to the stall.

Heather stood near the muck bucket. She held the leaking hose and her clothes dripped water onto the floor. Mascara ran from her eyes and gave her an authentic raccoon look. Her hair was plastered to her face and her T-shirt clung to her body.

"You," she sputtered, spitting water from her mouth. "Are so done."

I tiptoed toward her, trying not to laugh. "Heather, I'm so sorry. It was an accident."

She glared.

"If you want, you can wear my sweatshirt back to your

room," I offered. I didn't know whether to laugh or run screaming!

"I don't want your stupid sweatshirt," she said. Mascara drooled down her cheeks.

"You can hose me back if you want."

Heather brushed her sopping hair out of her face and let out a quick laugh. "Hose you? Right. I am going to do so much worse than hose you." Her eyes continued to glare back at me. For a second, I wished Mr. Conner would come back. A witness would be nice. But she just turned and headed out of the wash stall.

"It really was an accident," I called after her.

I fumbled in my pocket for my phone and pressed three wrong buttons before dialing Kim. Her answering machine picked up. "Kim? Can you please call me as soon as you get this? I'm not hurt and neither is Charm, so don't worry about that. Just call me."

I finished rinsing the buckets, put them away and headed for Charm's stall. Inside, I fed him an apple treat. He tickled my hands with his chin whiskers. At least Charm was happy to see me. "You need a trim, mister," I told him. I stepped up to his shoulder and grasped his mane with my left hand. With a hard push off the ground, I thrust myself onto his bare back. No halter, no saddle.

Just us. Leaning backward until my spine pressed against his back, I rested my head on his croup. "Six more days and then I'm going home," I told him.

Then I realized there was someone else I could call. She wasn't Kim, but she could listen. I dialed Callie.

"I hosed her," I said when Callie answered.

"What?" she asked.

"Heather. I was rinsing out a bucket after we finished mucking stalls, and I accidentally hosed her."

"Oh, my God, get over here and tell me in person! This sounds too good to tell over the phone."

"I'll be over soon," I promised.

"Don't forget a second of it," Callie said. "I want details!"

I closed my phone and smiled to myself. True, I was at the top of Heather's hit list. But I had a good friend in Callie, and good friends trump bratty mean girls.

13

THE NEW SASHA

THE SECOND WE HAD PULLED INTO THE garage last night, I'd raced into my room. Even though I knew everything would still be there, I was relieved Dad hadn't turned my room into a temporary gym or something. They had left all of my things in place, including my Breyer model horse collection that lined my desk, bookshelf, and window-sill. And best of all, I slept better than I had in weeks—*and* woke up to the smell of a home-cooked breakfast.

"Two weeks until the show," I told Mom and Dad as I ate my waffles. After three weeks at school, it was good to be home—I felt like I'd been at Canterwood forever. Last night, I'd wondered what Paige and Callie were doing and actually missed my dorm a little.

Mom checked the wall clock. "We've got to leave soon."

"I can't believe you're ditching us to visit Briar Creek," Dad teased.

I reached past him for the maple syrup. "Just for an hour. I have to say hello to Kim."

Mom wiped down the counter with a sponge.

"I took the day off so I could see both my girls," Dad said.

Mom and I put the dishes in the sink and headed out, leaving Dad strumming his air guitar and warbling some made-up country song about being lonely.

The trees outside had yellow and orange leaves. The road twisted and turned through the Connecticut country-side. It used to make me nauseous to dip and bend on the curvy roads, but now I loved it. Every twist brought me closer to Briar Creek.

The first thing I noticed when we got to Briar Creek was that the hunter course where I had cleared my first brush fence was gone. The grass, once torn by horseshoes, had grown back and there was no sign of the rustic jumps. I stood in the driveway and stared at the spot before heading inside.

Most of the students were in school, so the stables were quiet. "Hey, Irish!" I said, rushing up to the bay mare whose head hovered over the warped stall door. "Long time no see!" Irish whickered appreciatively as my fingers stroked her black muzzle and scratched her ear. Irish was the last horse I had ridden before my parents bought Charm. Irish, a tall horse at seventeen hands high, had been daunting to me when Kim helped me into her saddle for the first time. But we'd clicked. Within a couple of weeks, I'd taken home a trophy from a local hunt seat class.

I made my way down the narrow aisles, peering into the stalls of familiar horses. "Hi, Sherlock," I said to a fat sorrel pony a few stalls away from Irish. Sherlock was one of the many temperamental ponies I had ridden at Briar Creek. "I couldn't forget you," I said. "Not after you kicked me last summer." Sherlock kept his furry back to me and didn't look up when I left.

A few unfamiliar older girls, maybe in college, had horses crosstied in the aisle. I ducked under the crossties and headed for the back of the stable. I wondered whether or not my old friends even rode here anymore.

The more stalls I passed, the more unfamiliar horses I saw. Kim had at least a dozen new boarders. My chest twinged as I passed the hot walker and headed for Kim's office. It was small and cluttered—nothing like Mr. Conner's spacious air-conditioned office. But I'd missed it. "I'm *baa-ack*," I said, knocking on the door.

Kim turned around in her chair. "You're here!" She jumped up and grabbed me in a tight hug. "You look fantastic, hon."

"I really missed you!" I said.

"B.C. has changed a little, huh?" she asked.

"You have a lot of new boarders," I said,

Kim's gaze flitted to the piles of paper on her desk. "After you left, the team needed someone to replace you in the competitions. I added a dozen girls hoping one would stick and be able to fill your slot."

"Did you find one?"

Kim handed me a manila folder. "I did. Check out her file."

There was a photo paper clipped to the folder. A could-be magazine cover model looked back at me, her long brown hair hair peeking out from underneath a riding helmet. She looked about a year younger than me. "Lauren Towers," I read aloud. "Two-time national champion in juvenile show jumping and onetime dressage gold medalist at junior nationals." Better than me.

Kim grinned. "Impressive, huh? I was lucky to get her. Lauren could have started sixth grade at Canterwood, but she's not as mature as you. She wasn't ready to live twenty-four seven in that ultracompetitive environment." This time last year, Kim had been excited about me showing for Briar Creek. We'd spent dozens of late nights trotting around the arena on foot to pace out the jumps. Kim never missed one of my competitions. She probably made it to more shows than my parents.

"She seems perfect," I said.

"She takes direction well and she gets along with all of the riders."

"I'm happy the team is doing so great," I said. My fingers fiddled with the Briar Creek embosser on Kim's desk. "You're not upset that I left, are you?"

Kim twisted her chair away from the wall and stared at me. "Why in the world would I be upset?"

"You don't think I left you guys for something 'better' do you?"

Kim reached across the desk and patted my hand. "I *know* you left us for something better. I would have been upset if you'd stayed. There was nothing else for me to teach you. Your talents would have been wasted here. That's why I told you about Canterwood."

"It's weird riding for someone else," I said. "You've always been my instructor."

"Things change," Kim said. "One day, you'll look back on your time here and see it for what it was—a stepping stone. Do great at Canterwood—show people how much you learned here at B.C."

"I want you to have a great team," I said.

Kim locked eyes with me. "I know you do. And how are things with Heather and Aristocrat?"

"Never dull. Heather is like a green horse—unpredictable and uncontrollable."

Kim rolled her eyes.

"I'm trying to concentrate on Charm and the show," I said.

"That's the best way to deal with it," Kim said. "How *is* Charm doing with all of this?"

His name made me smile. "He's perfect. As always. He loves the stable and he gallops along the fence line whenever I turn him out."

"Sounds like he adjusted well, then."

"He has. I can't believe the show's in a week," I said.

"You're going to do great. I'll be visiting a farm in Lexington, but I know you'll tell me all about it."

"I will. We've been practicing at least six days a week," I said.

Kim looked at a framed photo of us, me sitting atop Charm's back, holding a blue ribbon. It was my first show with Charm in Union—and one of my favorite pictures.

"If you give Canterwood half of what you gave me, you'll never disappoint," Kim said.

"Thanks. Dad made Mom swear to pick me up in exactly one hour," I said, checking the time on my phone. "I better go."

Kim got up from her desk and wrapped me in a hug. It wasn't easy to picture me hugging Mr. Conner like this.

I left Kim to work in her office and headed for Charm's old stall for a quick peek. His nameplate was gone and the box stall was empty. The first time I had ridden Charm at Briar Creek rushed back to me. He balked at the first oxer and spooked before refusing the double rail. That day, I'd been afraid that Charm was wrong for me. But after a few weeks of practice, we had melded together.

I waited for Mom outside. The gravel crunched beneath my feet as I walked. I missed this place. But now, I missed my friends at Canterwood, too.

A couple of pastures away, a Welsh pony jumped fences as if they were nothing. Brown hair gleamed from underneath the white helmet. The horse leapt the last brush fence and the rider slowed the pony to a walk. The girl smiled and vigorously patted her mount's neck.

A sudden breeze picked up and blew through the trees. Reddish leaves floated down and dotted the ground. I pulled my cream-colored sweater tighter around my waist to ward off the chill. Mom's car pulled up the driveway and I got inside, not taking my eyes off Lauren. As we drove away, I turned in my seat and watched Briar Creek. It got smaller and smaller until it was nothing more than a speck in the rearview mirror.

14

JACOB LOVES · · ·
COTTON CANDY

SUNDAY AFTERNOON, AFTER MOM AND DAD
dropped me off at school, I ran straight to the stable to
see Charm. I couldn't stay long because Mr. Ramirez had
rescheduled Friday's film class for today.

I turned the corner and saw Alison standing by Charm's
stall. "Hey," I said. "What are you doing?"

Alison jumped back from the stall and yanked her
hands off the door. "Nothing. God, can't anyone walk by
your horse?"

I peered inside Charm's stall to be sure Alison hadn't
dumped manure inside or something.

"I've just never seen you around his stall before," I said.

"I just wanted to know how you do it." Alison shrugged.
She turned her back to the stall and leaned against the

door to face me. Her long, dark brown waves framed her perfectly made-up, heart-shaped face. "How do you get him so flexible?" She swallowed and looked at her boots. "Sunstruck isn't bending." She rolled her eyes. "Never mind."

"Take him through some pole bends," I said. "And lead him in tighter figure eights."

Alison smiled. Not a fake I-hate-you smile, either. "Maybe I'll try that," she said.

I entered Charm's stall and hugged his neck. "Alison asking for training advice," I murmured to him. Maybe Alison was getting nervous about the show, too.

I left the stall. Down the aisle, Nicole had Wish crosstied and Mr. Conner was bent over his hoof.

"Is he okay?" I asked Nicole.

"He's got a sore hoof," she said, her eyes filling with tears.

Mr. Conner stood and wiped his hands on his jeans. "It looks like a bruise, nothing too serious. But I'll call the vet and have her check him out."

"Can I still show?" Nicole whispered.

Mr. Conner shook his head and gave her a sympathetic look. "No, I'm sorry. Not on Wish. You could ride a school horse, if you want. I'll help you find a good fit."

Nicole sniffed back tears. I leaned over and squeezed her hand. "Wish will be okay," I said. "You could ride another horse at the show."

"No," Nicole said, patting Wish's neck. "I'll skip it. I can't leave him. It's just one show." But she looked as if she didn't believe it.

"I'm going to schedule Wish's appointment," Mr. Conner said. He left us and headed toward his office.

"Let's groom him and help make him feel better," I said.

Nicole nodded and handed me a body brush.

An hour later, I slid into my seat next to Jacob at film class.

Mr. Ramirez stepped in front of the class. "Let's get right to it. Homework. You will write a two-page paper on the strengths and weaknesses of dialogue in your assigned film. Half of you will watch *Gone With the Wind* and the rest will watch *Titanic*."

Mr. Ramirez handed out folded papers. "You may unfold your papers as soon as you receive one," he said.

Titanic was printed on my instruction sheet.

"What'd you get?" Jacob asked. He showed me his paper—*Titanic*.

"Same!" I said. *Okay*, I thought. *This would be a great time for Canterwood Sasha to step it up.* "Maybe we could help each other with our papers."

Jacob nodded. "Definitely."

OMG! Big yoga breath iiiiiiiiin and ouuuuuuuuuut.

"What's today's lip gloss?" Jacob asked.

I laughed and pulled one out of my backpack. "Cotton candy," I said. "Good or bad?"

He rubbed his hands together. "My favorite fairground food." He paused for a second. "So I was thinking—"

The roar of the MGM lion cut him off.

"What did you say?" I whispered.

"Nothing," he said. "I'll tell you later."

I faced the screen. What was he going to ask me?

CHARM GETS
A NEW 'DO

IT WAS SHOW DAY.

Early Saturday morning, Callie and I stood in front of the green and gold Canterwood horse trailers, trying to stay out of the grooms' way. The weak October sunlight wasn't enough to keep us warm. Mr. Conner even had some of the horses with thin coats in light blankets.

I ran my fingers over Charm's braids. The clear rubber bands were snug and my fingers ached from more than four hours of braiding. Livvie had let me stay with Charm until nine last night and I'd squinted in the faint light to give him perfect braids. That was part of our pre-show routine. Yesterday, Charm had a bath. His favorite shampoo and mane conditioner smelled like green apples. I worked the thick white formula into his mane, coat, and tail. After a quick rinse, I doused him with extra conditioner, careful not to get it in his eyes. He got a final rinse cycle, after taking a drink from the hose, and then I used the squeegee to remove excess water. Ever since our first show, I stayed late at the stable and groomed and bathed Charm for hours to make him look and feel his best. He always returned the favor and showed his hardest the next day.

Mr. Conner had begun to tell everyone where to load their horses. While we waited for directions, Callie and I led Jack and Charm through the wet grass and tried to keep them calm. It wasn't easy since riders dashed around—loading horses and carrying gear into the trucks.

I leaned over and plucked a piece of straw from Callie's French braid.

Black Jack yanked on the brown leather lead line. With the streetlamps shining behind him, he cast a long shadow over the grass. "Your parents are meeting you there, right?" Callie asked.

"Yeah—this is the longest they've gone without seeing me ride Charm."

Callie finished tightening Jack's leg wraps.

Across the lawn, Mr. Conner and two of the grooms had blindfolded Julia's mare, Trix, as they struggled to load her into the trailer. Mr. Conner gripped her black halter and gently tugged her forward. She took tiny steps up the ramp. Once inside, Mr. Conner got a groom to tie her and he headed in our direction.

"Morning, girls," he said. "Sasha, load Charm with Aristocrat. Callie, there's a spot next to Trix."

I walked Charm over to where Heather stood in full-out diva mode. Her shimmery nails gleamed. Her jeans were wrinkle free and her light pink hoodie was without a speck of horsehair. Alison rubbed her eyes as she passed by, trading a steaming hot chocolate for the PowerBar Heather munched. Julia dumped Heather's saddlebag and grooming kit on the grass beside the trailer.

"Don't put that on the ground, Jules!" Heather said. "I don't want dirt on my stuff." Heather rolled her eyes and whispered to Alison.

Julia picked up the gear and hauled it over to a table by the trailers.

I shoved my cold hands into my jacket pockets, wishing I were inside. It was still dark out, but the floodlights from the stable gave us just enough light.

I turned my attention to Charm. "Okay, boy. This one is yours. Ready to go inside?" Charm stretched his neck and eyed the trailer suspiciously. "You'll be fine. I'm here. Don't be scared." I leaned down and checked his leg wraps for the umpteenth time. Traveling with Charm always made me nervous. Trailer accidents were known to happen and it was hard for me to put Charm's life in a driver's hands. But I couldn't let him feel my nerves or he'd get upset. "Let's get inside." Clicking my tongue against the roof of my mouth, I urged Charm toward the trailer.

"That's Aristocrat's side. Move Charm to the right," Heather snipped. She strode to my side.

"Does it really matter?"

"It does, actually. Aristocrat doesn't travel well on the right side. Do you want me to get Mr. Conner so he can tell you that himself?"

"Fine, if it really bothers Aristocrat, Charm can ride on the right. He doesn't care what side he rides on."

"Whatever." Heather tugged on Aristocrat's lead line and headed for the trailer. Aristocrat stepped into the trailer as Heather tied him up. When she was done, she headed off with Julia and Alison. I noticed that Aristocrat's coat sparkled and in Aristocrat's side of the double trailer, Heather had given him a lot of extra lead.

Charm and I stepped up into the trailer. Mr. Conner had put rubber mats on the floor to prevent slipping. Aristocrat stretched his gleaming neck toward Charm and the two huffed at each other. Aristocrat turned his head away from Charm. Charm gave me a look that said *what a snob!*

"That's my boy," I said, patting his shoulder. At least Charm and I only had one class today. Mr. Conner had decided that since I was new, I'd show in my class and then assist him for the rest of the event.

I tied up Charm closer to the right side and patted him before getting out. On my way to the truck, my phone buzzed in my pocket.

Good luck today! Call me after U win! xoxo Paige

I texted back:

If not back by 8 = kidnapped by H. U get my dvds ;)

When we arrived, the four-trailer caravan pulled into the gravel unloading area for the Connecticut State Horse Show.

"What time is it?" I asked Callie as we climbed out.

"Seven fifteen," she said. "My class starts in forty-five minutes!"

We grabbed our duffel bags with our show clothes and dashed inside the blue and white check-in tent. We got our numbers—I drew 188 and Callie got 201—and followed signs to the changing areas to get ready.

The Connecticut State Horse Show was a big deal. Riders who won their divisions here could qualify for regional and national shows. At Briar Creek, I'd only done local shows—never state competitions. If Canterwood riders made it to regionals, we could travel anywhere in New England for a show. Most riders at the intermediate level showed at least once a month—some even every other weekend to get enough wins and points to qualify for bigger shows.

The fancy gold script painted on the Canterwood trailers was hard to miss. I buttoned on my choker, grabbed my bag and knocked on Callie's door.

"I'll be there in five minutes," Callie said. "My hairnet for dressage got tangled in my choker."

"Want help?" I shifted my bag and checked my watch. Twenty-nine minutes until Callie's class and mine was right after hers.

"Just go. Mr. Conner will notice if we're *both* gone."

I walked to the trailers. The sun had burned away the early morning fog. Horses and riders dotted the grounds.

Up ahead, I could see a warm-up ring tucked away behind the indoor arena. A metal sign pointed riders toward the cross-country course. Some of the fences were higher than my practice jumps. Trainers coached students on horseback and one instructor had her students doing pre-show Pilates on mats in the nearby field. The Canterwood trailers looked as big as tour buses. Mike was holding Charm's lead line in his hand. Charm wasn't moving.

"What's wrong?" I asked, my voice shaking. I ran my hands up and down Charm's legs.

"Sasha! Sasha!" Mike said, pulling me up. "He's fine. His legs are fine. Nothing's broken."

"What was wrong? I thought something happened!" Tears pricked my eyes as I stood and tried to steady myself against Charm's strong shoulder.

Mike shifted his eyes over to Charm's neck. I followed Mike's gaze to Charm's mane. Half of his once beautiful braids were gone. Stubs of mane stuck up in disarray. Mike offered me his hand. He held several of the braids, rubber bands still in place. After thinking Charm had hurt a leg, this was almost a relief. But I couldn't compete on a horse with a half-missing mane.

"It looks like Aristocrat is a chewer," Mike said. "Heather must not have tied him well enough. Looks like he tugged the knot loose and chewed on Charm's mane."

"Heather knew better," I said to Mike. "She put

Aristocrat on the left side because the tie ring was thicker and easier to tug loose. *I should have known better.*"

Mike started to say something when another student called him. "I'm sorry," he said, before jogging off to the unloading area.

Charm looked at me and I hugged him.

"I'm so sorry, boy," I said. "I'll get your mane fixed. Promise."

Callie dashed to my side, her helmet's unfastened chin strap flapping against her face. "Oh, Sasha. I'm so sorry. What can I do?"

"We've got to fix this before my class." I checked my watch. "In nineteen minutes! Can you grab me the clippers?"

Callie found the clippers in the supply bag. Starting at his withers, I buzzed off Charm's mane up to his ears leaving only his forelock. Poor Charm didn't move. The remaining braids fell to the ground. I'd tell Mom and Dad that a horse chewed off Charm's mane, but I wouldn't tell them Heather had let Aristocrat do it on purpose. There was already too much to deal with today.

A few yards away, Mom and Dad spotted me and waved. Um?

What was my mother wearing?! In one ear, she had a

green "C" earring and in the other she had a gold "A." How did she even find those? Dad had one hunter green croc on one foot and a gold croc on the other. His Nikon hung around his neck. The other parents who walked the grounds wore normal outfits like khakis, light-colored blouses and polo shirts. Not these Canterwood Crest Academy souvenir shop monstrosities!

Mom hugged me. Dad snapped at least ten pictures as he walked over. He should have been a paparazzo—not the manager of a regional bank.

"This is my friend Callie," I said.

"Hi, Callie," Dad said. "Are you riding with Sasha?"

"I have a different class in a few minutes," she said.

"Sasha!" Mom gasped, getting a look at Charm's mane.

Dad stepped around Mom and ran his hand over Charm's buzzed mane. "What happened?" he asked, lowering his camera.

"On the ride over, the horse next to him was trying to groom Charm and he accidentally bit too hard on the braids. I had to buzz off the rest."

"Oh, honey," Mom said. "Can he show like this?"

I nodded. "He'll be fine."

"I'm sorry that happened," Dad said. "But we know you'll do great anyway."

"Thanks, Dad. We should go, but I'll see you later."

"You going to tell them the truth?" Callie asked, once we were away from my parents.

"I don't want them to worry," I said.

Mike handed me Charm's bridle and took the halter. After a quick adjustment to Charm's girth, he was ready.

Alison rode up to us and leaned closer to me. "Thanks for the bending advice," she whispered, sneaking a glance at Heather, who was talking to Mr. Conner. "I think it worked."

"Good," I said. Callie gave me the wide-eyed, Alison's-talking-to-you look. Alison moved away from us and let Sunstruck walk over to Aristocrat.

"You're all going to do great," Mr. Conner said, giving us a rare smile. "I'm proud of each and every one of you."

I cheered as Callie gracefully dismounted and took Black Jack's reins in her free hand. Charm bobbed his head at Jack in congratulations.

"I can't believe I won first place!" Callie said, kissing her blue ribbon.

"You deserve it," I said, wondering if I'd ever have that silky blue prize in my hands.

Alison took her second place red ribbon and rammed it into her jacket pocket.

"The dirt on the drop fence was soft," Callie said. She loosened Jack's saddle and followed me off the outdoor course. "It's softer than it should be. We almost stumbled on the landing—that's what took Alison down."

Callie looked so professional in her dressage habit—black top hat, thigh-high boots and fitted jacket. Regulations for dressage were strict. Perfecting all of the moves Callie practiced so many times didn't look easy.

My class started in half an hour—time for one final warm-up.

"Riders of the stadium jumping intermediate class round two, please proceed to ring number four. Number 187, Julia Myer, you're up first." Charm and I waited just outside the ring while my class started. Mom and Dad waved at me from the stands.

I adjusted my crooked black helmet. I shouldn't have goofed off so much with Paige last week. Instead of watching a movie marathon on the Disney Channel, I should have been in the stables pacing out my jumps and working with Charm!

The loudspeaker crackled to life. "Score for number

187, Julia Myer, is no faults. Number 188, Sasha Silver, please enter the ring."

Julia had a perfect score—zero.

When I squeezed my legs, Charm walked forward. The high jumps looked more daunting with every step he took. We stood at the edge of the ring while I took one final breath. A clear round was the only way to stay in the game.

The jumps—including planks and a combination—seemed to stretch into the top of the indoor ceiling. They looked menacing. During practices, Mr. Conner had gradually increased the jump heights and built up the team by teaching us how to approach tall jumps. Still, these obstacles were a couple of inches higher than Canterwood's rails. The goal was to make it cleanly over the jumps and not to go over time. If I did, I'd pick up a penalty.

We waited for the starting bell. My head felt hot under my helmet. My slick hands gripped the reins. The bell rang out. On my go, Charm surged forward and our time began.

Charm sailed over the first small vertical and pulled at the bit to head for the red and white oxer. "Easy," I soothed. "Nice and slow." He flicked his ears back for a second, listening to my voice, and then tucked his legs gracefully under his body and cleared the second jump. We made a long half circle and cantered to the third and fourth jumps, a quick in and out. We needed to clear the third jump and leave the ground one stride later to leap the fourth. My breath stopped as Charm collected himself, slowed, and landed perfectly between the third and fourth fence. He skyrocketed over the fourth fence, with a dizzying triangle pattern, and surged forward to the water jump.

"Not so fast," I whispered. "Slow down." I gave the reins a few short, sharp tugs, to try to slow his pace. Water jumps—or liverpools—were tricky. The fake water below often scared horses if they approached wrong.

I did a half-halt—pulling slightly on the reins while urging Charm forward with my seat. But he continued to barrel toward liverpool. He wasn't listening! If I didn't do something, he could injure a leg when he landed on the other side. With my forgotten gloves in the trailer, the reins cut into the skin between my thumb and finger. The only option was to ride *with* him instead of against him. We swept past the judges. My grip on the reins relaxed and I gave Charm his head to approach the jump as he wanted. I prayed we wouldn't knock the rail.

Hoofbeats thudded in my ears. My hands slid along Charm's neck as we approached the jump. His body lifted into the air, clearing the rail. He seemed to suspend over the water. I took a gulp of air when his hooves hit the dirt. Thank God! His left front leg wobbled as he hit a soft patch and I held still to give him the room to correct his landing. Charm's back hooves landed centimeters away from the water line. He cantered to the final jumps.

We made it around the next few jumps without knocking down a rail or brushing a fence. Excitement bubbled inside me, as I focused on finishing the course.

The final obstacle was a rustic wooden rail with boxes of bright flowers on the sides. The flowers were meant to distract the horse and cause the horse to refuse the jump. Charm cantered vigorously toward the jump and surged over it. His hoof thudded against the rail and I twisted around to see the rail shudder in place before staying in the hold. Yes! I'd just tied with Julia! She was by the arena fence, talking furiously into her cell phone.

"Number 188," the loudspeaker said. "Sasha Silver has a score of no faults." I let out a whoop of excitement, dismounted, and led Charm out of the arena.

"Look at that, boy!" I said to Charm. "We cleared all of those jumps!" Charm flexed his neck, pawing the ground. Mom and Dad whistled from the stands.

And then it hit me: Julia and I were going head-to-head.

16

TWO BLUE RIBBONS, FOUR GIRLS, AND SOME SERIOUS ATTITUDE

THE LAST RIDER FINISHED HIS ROUND. JULIA and I stood on opposite sides of the ring, waiting to hear his score. "Number 196, Alex Walker, has scored zero faults," the announcer said.

My heart pounded. It was official: Julia, Alex and I would compete in the jump-off. We'd have the same course, we'd be competing for the fastest time, and the rails would be raised in this round. The judges removed two verticals from the course. Our jumping order was determined randomly—Alex had the first slot, followed by Julia and then me.

I watched Alex's ride. His black gelding, Agent Ace, thundered over the jumps and Alex urged him into a slow gallop on the long turns. The final jump was the highest of the course, but Alex and Ace soared over it. The crowed roared its approval.

"Final time for Alex Walker is fifty-nine seconds with no faults," said the announcer.

Julia mounted Trix. She had to jump clean and beat Alex's time. A bell sounded. The bay mare seemed to have the course memorized. Julia's face never changed expression—she kept her eyes forward, always on the jump ahead of her. She urged Trix into a fast canter as they approached the final jump. Trix leapt into the air and at the last second, her shiny black hoof nicked the rail. The rail shook and looked as if it would bounce out of the holder and tumble into the dirt. Julia looked over her shoulder as the rail wobbled and then settled back into the hold. My stomach sank. Audience applause filled the ring and Julia pumped her fist in victory. That was going to be hard to beat.

"Time for Julia Myer is fifty-two seconds with no faults."

Julia trotted over to me. "Are you really going to even try?"

Her face was half hidden by her black riding helmet. She had a few splotches of arena dirt on her nose. I ignored her and double-checked Charm's bell boots.

"Heather!" Julia called across the ring. Heather ran over and high-fived Julia. A red ribbon—second place—peeked out of her jacket pocket.

"Is that the new It look, Silver? A buzzed mane?" Heather asked, smirking.

Charm swung his hindquarters around so Heather got a lovely shot of chestnut rump. Before I could say a word, Julia and Heather linked arms and took Trix to the waiting area. Julia draped Trix in a sweat sheet and waited to watch my round.

I turned away from them, focusing all my attention on Charm. Glancing into the stands, I saw Callie waving a blue ribbon at me. She beat Heather in dressage! With a grin, I gave her a thumbs up before signaling Charm to enter the ring. Charm stepped up to the starting line and the bell sounded.

I pushed Charm into a fast canter as we cleared the first jump. He landed easily and huffed in excitement as he powered toward the second fence.

Charm slowed a notch and the oxer was soon behind us. He soared over the rails, the water jump and the in and out set. I urged him into a slow gallop on the long turn and we approached the final rail and the evil flower box. We hadn't knocked a rail yet, but I couldn't tell if our time was faster than Julia's. Charm gathered himself before the final fence and we flew over it. His hooves pounded the dirt after the jump.

Leaning down, I rubbed his sweaty neck. "Way to go, boy!"

Charm trotted out of the ring. Julia and Alex led their horses beside Charm as we waited for my time.

"Nice ride," Alex said as I dismounted.

I smiled at him. "Thanks! You, too." At least the guys at St. Alexander's School for Boys seemed decent. But not as cute as Jacob.

No one spoke to Julia as she stared straight ahead and didn't look at any of us. The loudspeaker came on. We all held our breaths.

"Number 188, Sasha Silver." Please, oh, please. "Time is fifty-five seconds with no faults."

Cheers erupted from the ring. I'd lost by three seconds! I let out my breath and slumped against Charm's side. The only class at my first state show and I didn't win. Charm flicked back his ears, looking at me for reassurance, and I patted his neck. "It's okay, boy. You did great." I knew it wasn't his fault. If I had worked harder on timing, we'd be taking that blue ribbon. We would have to practice more, or there was no way we'd make the advanced team.

I looked into the stands. Mom and Dad, standing in their seats, cheered as if I had won first place.

With a sigh, I led Charm over to Julia and tried to smile. "Congratulations," I said. "It was a good round."

"I don't need your congratulations," Julia spat. Mr. Conner motioned Julia over to him and she headed off, leaving me alone.

"Charm, I'm so sorry," I said to him. "We would have won if I'd practiced more."

Charm watched me and nosed my arm. He didn't look as defeated as I felt.

"Your first show at this easy level and you didn't win," Heather said. "Poor Sasha Silver from Briar Creek." She reached past me and stroked Charm's buzzed mane. I held myself back from slapping her hand away. Instead, I led Charm away. I collected my red ribbon from the judge and pinned it on Charm's bridle. I consoled myself that Mom, Dad, and Callie had seemed thrilled that we'd gotten second place. Maybe they thought that's the best I could do.

"Aren't you going to go do a victory dance with Julia?" I asked Heather later while we waited for the horses in front of us to exit so we could leave.

"Why would I do that when I can stay here with you?" Heather asked, not even glancing in Julia's direction. I looked at Heather's ribbon. "If you think it's because she won and I didn't, you're wrong. There were actually talented riders in *my* class."

"So, what happened? Why aren't you with Julia, then?"

Heather kicked her boot into the arena dirt.

For a second, she had that same look as when she had fought with her father in the parking lot. I couldn't help feeling a surge of sympathy.

"I know it's tough sometimes," I said. "But—"

"Do you think I need advice from *you*?" Heather interjected. "I have my own friends, so save it for someone else." She walked right past Julia, who was posing for a photo with Mr. Conner, holding up her blue ribbon. That could have been Charm and me.

The horses in front of me separated and I led Charm out of the arena. We waited for my parents outside.

"Way to go, honey," Dad said, squeezing my arm.

"Second place!" My mom enthused.

They were beaming with pride. I felt ungrateful, suddenly, and guilty about the way I'd reacted to their clothes. "I'm so glad you guys are here."

We took our time walking to the trailers. I listened to Mom and Dad chatter about the way "Charm attacked that fence."

"Want to grab a soda with us before you help Mr. Conner?" Dad asked.

"That sounds good," I said. I was grateful to have a few more minutes before we had to say good-bye.

Mom seemed to sense my mood. "We'll be seeing you in a couple of weeks for Parents' Weekend," Mom reminded me.

I nodded, but even that didn't make me feel much better. When Charm and I got back to Canterwood, we were going to practice. School and fun couldn't get in the way. This show was over. Now it was all about the advanced team. Charm and I had five weeks to work. If people thought I practiced hard before, they hadn't seen anything yet. I could balance good grades and practice like crazy.

It wasn't even a choice—I had to.

17

SASSY SILVER
SCORES BIG

I ABSENTMINDEDLY STIRRED MY SODA WITH my bendy straw and stared out the cafeteria window. A week had passed since the show and I was still feeling down.

Julia had gloated all week long about her blue ribbon. She brought it everywhere—to lunch, to practice—even to class. Callie was excited about her wins, too, even though she downplayed it for my benefit. Paige did her best to cheer me up. She'd even gotten permission from Livvie to make chocolate-chip pancakes this morning, since it was a Saturday. At least Parents' Weekend was a week away— thinking about showing Mom and Dad around campus gave me something else to focus on.

Charm was sad, too. He seemed listless in his stall and when I turned him out in the pasture, he ambled around instead of taking his usual gallop up and down the fence. Charm wasn't used to losing.

I had to focus all of my energy on practicing for the advanced team testing before Thanksgiving break.

"Hey, Sasha." Jacob slid into the empty seat next to me. He looked cuter than the last time I saw him—if that was possible.

"Hey, Jacob. Aren't we lucky that we got *Titanic* for our homework assignment?"

"Especially since *Gone with the Wind* is so long," he said

We were trying to figure out who had seen more classic movies. Jacob had sworn he was the winner, but I had one-upped him when he had admitted he'd never seen *The Sound of Music*. Jacob stole a barbecue chip off my plate. "I'm having trouble with my paper, though."

"Really?" I asked. "If you want any help . . . ,"

"You wouldn't mind?" Jacob had no trace of a smile on his face. "I kind of suck at papers."

"I could read what you have and give you some pointers," I offered, trying to stay calm.

"That would be great!" A smile lit his face. "And, uh," his voice cracked. "Maybe if you're not busy now, and you probably are, we could get ice cream. Or something. If you want."

Color crept into my face. I fumbled around in my pocket for my lip gloss and tried not to make eye contact. *Say something.* "Sure," I said, between yoga breaths.

We left the cafeteria and headed for the ice cream shop near the Canterwood Media Center.

"Have you had the initiation ice cream yet?" Jacob asked, looking at me as we ignored the "stay off the grass" signs and took a shortcut over the springy Canterwood lawn.

"What is that?" I asked. "It sounds kind of scary."

"It sounds disgusting, but you have to try it." His green eyes gleamed. "It's mint chocolate chip with caramel sauce—Canterwood's colors. It's really not that bad."

"I'll try it," I said, hoping I sounded adventurous.

When we reached the ice-cream shop, we stepped up to the counter.

"Two cones with mint chocolate chip ice cream and caramel sauce, please," Jacob said to the server.

A few minutes later, we got our cones. "Cheers," he said, tapping his cone to mine. I took a tiny bite.

"Wow, it's really good!" I said.

"Yeah, it just sounds gross," Jacob said smiling. We left the shop and walked past the library. Soon, we ended up by the English building and our ice cream was long gone. Neither of us had said a word for a few minutes. I pulled my sweater over my chilly fingers, trying to think of something interesting to talk about.

"Well," I said. "Thanks for initiating me."

"Anytime." Jacob twisted the leather bracelet on his arm. "Do you want to come with me to the center to play video games?"

After my loss at the show, I probably should have been at the stables practicing, but taking a break for an hour was probably okay. And anyway, Charm was grazing outside and he deserved a rest.

"Sure," I said, finally.

"Ever played before?" Our arms bumped together when I stepped on an uneven part of the sidewalk.

"You'll have to teach me," I said.

The video game room was empty. "Is Super Smash Brothers Brawl okay?" Jacob asked.

"Sure, whatever you want." I tried to figure out where to sit. Did I plop down on the floor with a pillow? Or perch on the couch with one leg crossed like Paige did? Jacob put the disc into the console and sat cross-legged on the floor. I sat a couple of feet away from him and mirrored his casual posture.

He handed me a white controller. "I'll teach you." He

leaned over, so I could smell his sweet, minty breath, and arranged my fingers on the controller. My cheeks burned. Jacob Schwartz was touching me! A boy was touching my fingers! No more hand washing. Ever. An endless row of exclamation points shot through my brain.

Jacob turned on the TV and the game started. "First, pick a character," he said. Jacob chose a setting for us to play. "Okay, your goal is to press the A and B buttons and knock me off the screen. Got it?"

I looked over at him and, for a second, our eyes met. The game clock counted down and on "Go!" we started to battle. Pressing every button, I maneuvered Yoshi around the screen and tried to look as if I knew what I was doing. I glanced at Jacob. It seemed like he didn't care if I was a good player or not. He just wanted to have fun.

With me.

After a while, we took a break to give our thumbs a rest. He handed me a slip of folded notebook paper.

I opened it. *GamerGuy.* "What's this?" I asked.

"It's my IM name," he said. "So . . . maybe we can chat sometime."

"Cool," I said.

!!!!!!!!!!

I tore off a strip of paper from his note, wrote *SassySilver* and handed it to him. "That's mine."

An hour later, practically floating, I headed for the exit and dialed Paige.

I squealed into the phone.

"Oh, my God, tell me!" Paige shrieked.

"It was amazing. We had ice cream and played video games."

"You're so lucky," Paige said with a sigh. "Why aren't there any cute boys in my cooking class?"

"We'll find you one," I said. "See you in a bit." I clicked the phone shut.

I stared at my fingers, half expecting them to glow or show some sign that Jacob had touched them. I went back to Winchester, waiting the whole way for my hands to glow.

18

THE FOXES AND THE
SILVERS: ONE BIG,
UNHAPPY FAMILY

"MY PARENTS WILL BE HERE IN AN HOUR!"
Paige squeaked. She raced to my side of the room, nearly
tripping over the vacuum, and stood on my bed. Paige had
been up since five, cleaning.

Parents' Weekend had taken over Canterwood Crest
Academy. Across the hall, Livvie was dispersing cleaning
products to residents as they prepped for parental invasion.
This weekend was going to be a busy one.

"You're making me feel bad," I said to Paige. "You're
running around and I'm not doing anything."

She climbed on my bed and started peeling off the
Hunter poster.

"What are you doing?" I cried. "Not Hunter!" I grabbed her
fuzzy, blue, sock-clad foot, and tried to pull her off my bed.

"A man poster can't stare at them when they walk in the door!" She peeled off the tape, carefully folded Hunter and slid him under my bed.

High heels clicked up and down the hallways. Parents knocked on dorm room doors. I heard Livvie telling someone's mother, "Of course she brushes her teeth every night!"

Mom and Dad would be meeting me in the courtyard any minute. I knew they would want to visit Charm, but what if we ran into the Trio? Mom and Dad still didn't know about them—and I didn't want them to worry. Luckily, we wouldn't have much time to spend in the stable since Canterwood had practically scheduled every single second of Parents' Weekend.

"I'm heading out to meet my parents," I said to Paige. "See you later!" I hurried out of Winchester and headed down the sidewalk.

"Sashie!" Mom sang from across the courtyard. I cringed.

Another girl was doing the same thing a few feet away.

A man who looked like her father had just yelled, "Here we are, princess!" We exchanged a look of mutual discomfort.

"I can't wait for Parents' Weekend to be over," she said in a hurried whisper. "Every year I tell them Parents' Weekend is cancelled and every year they find out I'm lying."

Her parents got to her first and swooped her in a hug. She tried to gracefully untangle herself from them before anyone noticed. But when she pulled away, she didn't let go of her mom's hand.

In seconds, Mom and Dad reached me and wrapped me up in a hug.

"I missed you guys," I said, taking in Dad's familiar woodsy scent.

"We missed you," Mom said, pulling me in for another hug. "We thought Parents' Weekend would never come!"

I extracted myself from her arms. "Paige can't wait to meet you guys!"

"Lead the way," Dad said.

I sighed with relief that there was no camera hanging from his neck.

Inside the dorm, Mom pointed to an ad on the board and Dad put his sunglasses on top of his head to read it. "'Come join the Frisbee club.'" Yet another one of Utz's activities. "'Flying fun for everyone.' You would have loved that club in school, wouldn't you, Gail?"

Mom shook her head. "Frisbee would have been better than Latin. I would have been so much cooler!"

"As a former football jock, sweetheart, I'm telling you that Frisbee Club wouldn't have made you any less dorky," Dad said.

"Ouch," she replied, matching his grin.

We headed down the hallway and stopped at my open door.

Paige waved my parents inside. "Welcome, Mr. and Mrs. Silver! I'm so happy to finally meet you." She hugged Mom and shook Dad's hand. "Can I offer you some hot mulled cider from our dorm kitchen?"

"Oh, you don't have to make us cider," Mom said, hugging Paige back. "Sasha has told us about you, too. The dorm looks great!"

"Thank you, Mrs. Silver!" Paige beamed.

"Are these lemon squares?" Mom asked, looking at the prettily arranged yellow squares on the coffee table.

"Those sure are lemon squares," Paige said. "Help yourselves."

"Are your parents coming?" Dad asked her.

"They should be here soon," Paige said.

"We look forward to meeting them," Mom said. Paige headed for our closet and grabbed her jacket.

"I have a few errands to run before my parents get here. I'll see you guys later!" Paige said.

"It sounds like you two are getting along well," Mom said.

I sat on Paige's bed. "We're getting along great. I've heard roommate horror stories, but I really got lucky with Paige. I can't wait to meet her parents."

"What do they do?" Dad asked.

"They own a restaurant in New York City and her dad's also in real estate."

"That sounds interesting," Dad said as he paged through my algebra textbook. He tried to mentally figure out one of the answers and I grinned when he looked stumped. Canterwood math frazzled even my banker dad!

"Do you want a tour before Paige's parents get here?" I asked, brushing a stray horsehair off my jeans.

"That sounds great!" Mom said. She grabbed her purse from my bed and Dad eased himself out of my chair.

I showed Mom and Dad the coffee shop, cafeteria, gym, and bowling lanes, but then I started to run out of ideas.

"I want to see Charm," Mom said, sidestepping a small pile of leaves. "I haven't seen him since the show.

"Okay," I chirped. "He'd love to see you guys."

At least I didn't have to worry about running into

the Foxes. Callie had heard through the grapevine that Heather's parents were on vacation in Bermuda.

We entered the stable and headed down to Charm's stall. The quiet aisles had only a few students milling around with their parents. "Charm is so happy," I said. "He loves his deluxe stall."

"He *should* love it. It's the size of the old ring at Briar Creek," Dad said.

I unlatched Charm's door.

"He's toned up so much recently," I said. "He can canter without getting tired for fifteen minutes longer than he could last year and his gaits are so much smoother—"

A fuzzy, familiar pony named Royal stood inside Charm's stall. Charm's bucket and hay net were gone.

"Where's Charm, hon?" Dad asked. "Is this the wrong stall?"

"No," I snapped. "This is Charm's stall." When I reached to grab Royal's halter, the palomino pony flattened his ears against his head and showed the whites of his eyes. I jerked my hand back and slammed the door shut.

"Did Charm get moved?" Mom asked, peering into the stalls next to Royal. "Should we go find Mr. Conner?"

"It's a joke that some of us play on each other," I said. "This pony bites and it's a pain to move him around."

"Oh," Mom said, "that's a cute tradition."

"Wait here a sec," I said. I stepped away from the stall. "Let me check down here for Charm." While Mom and Dad read the nameplates of Charm's stable mates, I jogged down the aisle, glancing in the stalls.

Black Jack, Trix, Sunstruck, and Aristocrat were all in their own stalls. Royal's stall was empty. Finally, I spotted a chestnut back. I dashed up to the stall. "Charm!" A horse that was definitely not Charm turned and looked at me. He swept his ears back and turned his back on me. I zigzagged across the aisle to check the remaining stalls. I was going to kill her. Familiar ears stuck up from a stall to my left. "Oh, Charm," I said. I waved my parents over. "Here he is."

"I can tell you've been working him," Dad said. "He looks amazing!"

Charm's chiseled legs had new muscles running from his knees to his hooves. He had lost his slight hay belly. I smiled, but kept my attention directed toward Royal's stall. Heather would surely return to the scene of the crime.

"How many hours a week are you riding now?" Dad

gently stroked Charm's soft muzzle. Charm leaned into Dad's hand.

"Twenty to twenty-five." Out of the corner of my eye, I watched Heather saunter her way to Royal's stall. "Can you wait here? I need to speak to my friend for a minute." I tore off down the aisle.

"That was too much," I said to Heather.

"Let's not be all dramatic," Heather said, smoothing her skirt.

I stomped in the direction of Mr. Conner's office and yelled over my shoulder. "I'm over this," I said. "I'm telling Mr. Conner that you moved Charm out of his stall."

I knocked on Mr. Conner's office door and, before he could call me inside, I pushed it open. A thin woman with dyed blond hair sat in one of Mr. Conner's chairs. "Sasha," Mr. Conner said. "I'm in a meeting at the moment. Is this an emergency?"

"Yes, Mr. Conner! Heather moved Charm into a different stall. She took all of his gear and put him at the end of the stable."

Mr. Conner raised his hand, "Wait a minute, Sasha—"

"She did," I said, cutting him off. "She stuck Royal in his stall and I can't get him out because he bites."

He gave a thin-lipped smile to the woman sitting in the chair. The woman's posture stiffened and she brushed off her fitted beige jacket as she stood. "Sasha," Mr. Conner warned. "We'll talk about this later."

"Mr. Conner, Charm could have been hurt—"

Heather sidestepped me and slipped her arm around the waist of the tall woman in Mr. Conner's office. "Sasha can't take a little joke between friends sometimes," Heather said.

A familiar-looking man stepped into the office behind Heather.

I was trapped in Mr. Conner's office with the Foxes!

I should have known Heather's parents wouldn't pass up the chance to grill Mr. Conner about her progress. Mr. Fox couldn't have been happy after Heather's loss to Callie at the state show.

"William," Mrs. Fox said to Mr. Conner, as she adjusted the diamond tennis bracelet on her wrist. "What's going on?" I couldn't believe I had ranted about Heather in front of her parents.

"I'm not sure," Mr. Conner said. "But we're certainly going to find out." He turned back to me. "Where are your parents?"

"At Charm's stall."

Heather's mother slung an arm over her daughter's shoulder. They looked like sisters.

Mr. Conner motioned for me to step out. "Why don't you bring them in."

Ten minutes later, with formal, stuffy greetings behind us, the Foxes and the Silvers sat side by side in Mr. Conner's office.

"What's going on?" Mom asked Mr. Conner. "Is there a problem?" Poor Mom and Dad. I had dragged them in here without saying anything except that I'd explain the whole thing later. Mom looked as if we had been called to the principal's office.

Mr. Conner folded his hands and placed them on the desk. "I'm not sure *what* the problem is, Mrs. Silver. Heather? Sasha?"

Heather clicked her Sidekick shut and smiled. "There's no problem, Mr. Conner. I played a harmless little trick on Sasha. I guess because she was stressed about Parents' Weekend, she got upset." Heather glanced at me out of the corner of her eye.

Mr. Fox's cell phone rang and he jumped up to answer it. "Sorry," he said to us, covering the phone with his hand. "I've got to take this." Mrs. Fox ignored him and kept her eyes on Heather.

"Sasha? Is that true?" Mr. Conner asked.

I glanced at Mrs. Fox, her skin stretched tight over her face. She raised her eyebrows and gave me an all-too-familiar stare.

"There is something I should confess," I said slowly, watching Heather's face. Her mouth pressed into a tight line.

"Mr. Conner, whatever she says, it's not true," Heather interjected.

"You mean it's not true that you offered to make a truce?" I said in a pretend surprised tone.

"Of course *that's* true," she said, her sweet tone returning. "I thought I'd try to make things better between us since we got off on the wrong foot."

"She did," I said. "She said she'd even muck Charm's stall this week as a peace offering. Wasn't that generous?" I struggled to keep a straight face. She had no way out of this one.

"That was kind of you, Heather," Mr. Conner said with a hint of a smile. "I'll let Mike know that you'll be caring for Charm this week."

I kept my eyes on Mr. Conner, avoiding Heather's glare. Charm was getting extra bran all week as an added bonus for his substitute groom.

Mrs. Fox stood, her legs stretching for miles in expensive-looking high heels, and motioned for Heather to follow her. "We have a dinner we need to attend, but we'll speak with you later, I'm sure." Heather and Mrs. Fox slipped out of the office.

Dad got to his feet and extended his hand to Mr. Conner. "I hope that's as serious as the pranks get around here," Dad said as he shook Mr. Conner's hand.

I inched toward the door.

"Mom," I said, tugging on her sleeve. "We should go. I don't want to be late to meet Paige."

"My riders are usually quite serious about why they're here," Mr. Conner said. "I hope the pranks are out of their system now." My ears reddened and I nodded. "Sasha, I'll see that Charm gets back to his stall." He tipped his head at us and we shuffled out of his office.

When we left the stable, Mom and Dad didn't say a word. Dad pointed out a picnic table under a large oak tree. "Sasha, we need to talk," he said.

"Let's talk later," I smiled. "If we don't go, we'll be late."

"Then we'll be late. Sit." Mom wasn't kidding.

Dad took a seat on the bench and Mom sat beside him, placing her fancy purse, the one she only used for weddings and visits to Canterwood, beside her.

"What's going on?" Dad asked. He looked as if he already knew.

Part of me was still their little girl and wanted my mom to step in to fix everything. But I was twelve, not five. "Nothing," I said.

"Tell us," Mom said, her voice soothing.

I sat in silence.

"Heather and I just don't get along," I said, finally.

"Why?" Dad asked.

"She thinks I'm going to make the advanced team instead of her," I said.

Mom and Dad exchanged a look. "Think of it as a compliment," Mom said. "Heather must think you're a really good rider if she's worried about you."

"It's more than that," I said. "She's tried everything to get me to leave!"

Dad took off his sunglasses. "Like what?"

I sighed. "Stupid pranks like the thing with Royal and she tried to mess me up at the show."

Mom's eyes narrowed on me. "Did Heather do something to ruin Charm's mane at the show?"

I nodded.

Mom snatched her purse from the table and started to stand. "I'm going back to talk to Mr. Conner," she said. "This has got to stop."

"No!" I grabbed her arm. "You can't do that, Mom. If

you go in there, things with Heather will get even worse. I've made it this far, haven't I? Sooner or later, Heather will give up and realize I'm not quitting." I hope I sounded more sure than I felt.

Slowly, Mom inched back onto the wooden bench. The angry pink faded from her face. "Are you sure? Dad and I could talk to Mr. Conner."

"I'm sure," I said. "I don't want to spend the rest of the weekend talking about Heather. We have dinner with Paige and her parents. Let's go meet them."

Mom reached across the table and grabbed my hand. "You have to promise to call us if this gets out of hand."

"Promise," I said, relaxing my shoulders. "Let me call Paige and let her know we're on our way." I reached into my pockets and got nothing but crumbs from an old horse treat. "My phone must be in the barn. Can we meet back at Winchester and then walk to the dining hall together?"

Dad checked his watch. "We'll see you in a bit."

I ran back to the stable. I rounded the corner by Mr. Conner's office and halted when I heard a man's angry voice. I hung back and peered around the corner.

"When are you going to grow up?" Mr. Fox's voice rang out. "This is just a waste of time and money if you're not going to focus on the team."

"I'm sorry, Dad." Heather looked like a scared little kid with her eyes glued to the barn floor. "I *am* focusing, I promise. I won't let you down."

"You lost at a *state show*," Mr. Fox said. "How do you expect to do at nationals? And what about the team at school?"

"I'll make it," Heather said. "Don't worry."

"If you don't show improvement, we're pulling you out of Canterwood Crest Academy and selling the horse. This is the last—" Mr. Fox started and was cut off by his insistent cell phone ring. "Go," he said to her. "We'll finish this later." Mr. Fox moved off down the aisle. His loud voice made even the horses nervous.

I pretended to be reading a flier about the Halloween miniature horse auction next week. Heather rounded the corner and almost ran into me.

"You okay?" I asked.

Heather pushed past me. Her eyes were red and swollen. "Stop pretending like you care!"

Even Heather didn't deserve the way her father treated her. I cut through the indoor arena to reach Charm's stall. Mike or someone else had already moved him back and Royal was gone. I spotted my phone and grabbed it off the rack. I started away from the door, but turned back to him. "You okay? Sleepy?" I asked. He swished his tail and stepped up to the stall door. He put his chin in my cupped hands and I kissed his muzzle. "I love you, boy. Wish me luck." It was almost time to meet the Parkers.

19

MEET THE PARKERS

THE DINING HALL HAD BEEN TRANSFORMED for Parents' Weekend with new table linens, blooming orange zinnias and freshly mopped floors.

The student maitre d' led us past the families spread among round tables with floor-length tablecloths. Candles on each table emitted a warm yellow light—a nice contrast from the harsh fluorescent ones that usually lit the room. I spotted Paige and waved.

A pretty blond woman with soft curls stood and squealed when she saw me. "Ooooh, you must be Sasha! I'm Mrs. Parker." She wrapped her arms around me as her lilac perfume washed over me. She stepped back and touched my elbow with her hand. "Oh, dear, you're just as lovely as Paige said you were. Richard," Mrs. Parker called to a man at the table who had red hair just like Paige's. "This is Sasha and these are her parents, Gail and Jim."

With a wide smile, Mr. Parker stood and shook my hand. "Nice to meet you," he said. "We've heard loads about you."

Within minutes, the dads were deeply engrossed in basketball talk.

"I have a few ideas for you girls," Mrs. Parker said to Paige and me. "I drew up the plans to rearrange your furniture. It will give you more space to entertain! If you throw a party in your dorm, you've got to have room."

"Oh, what a nice idea!" Mom chimed in.

Paige and I shot each other a knowing glance.

Mrs. Parker reached into her large bag and drew out a laminated sheet of paper. "This is a small list of things you girls could do to add fun and functionality to your room. I wrote it out in my spare time."

"Mom," Paige said, her tone impatient. "We like the dorm the way it is."

"Just look at my list," Mrs. Parker said as she laid the paper on the table.

"Bathroom, closets, and general space," I read aloud. The list was divided into color-coded sections with suggestions for improvement in each of those areas.

"The shower definitely needs caddies," Mrs. Parker said. "I've made one for each of you. I was going to save them as Christmas gifts for you girls, but I'll just have to make something else for the holidays." Mrs. Parker smiled sweetly.

"I think the caddies are a lovely idea, Celia," Mom chimed in. "I always wished for crafty bones. I'm barely able to handle scissors."

Mrs. Parker clinked her glass to my mom's as laughter erupted from the men's end of the table. Dad gestured emphatically with his hands while he marveled that Mr. Parker got more sports channels—twenty-seven to be exact—than he did.

I looked over at the other tables and saw Heather sitting with Mr. and Mrs. Fox. No one spoke. Heather stared at her plate of grilled chicken and swirled her fork in her corn. She looked as if she wanted to disappear.

We ordered our meals and within twenty minutes, steaming plates of grilled salmon and lemon chicken arrived.

"Do you girls have any big events coming up soon?" Dad asked while he sipped his coffee.

"We have a charity auction for miniature horses next weekend on Halloween," I said.

The adults nodded and smiled.

"I've got a gardening seminar off campus that weekend," Paige said. "I can't wait!"

Mrs. Parker beamed.

"What are your plans after dinner?" Mom asked Mrs. Parker.

"Unfortunately, we're due back home, but we had a lovely visit with Paige. Didn't we, darling?"

Paige nodded. "We did, Mom."

"Oh, before I forget," Mrs. Parker said, "I've got to show you this. Now, if you look at my diagram, which is drawn to scale, if you each move your bed five centimeters in opposite directions, you'll have more room around your coffee table." Paige and I peered harder at the diagram. That didn't sound so bad. Maybe we should both embrace the reigning queen of dorm décor.

By the time the waiters brought out the apple cobbler, Paige and I had promised to move our beds and send Mrs. P. a picture of the updated room.

"I'll call you, Gail," Mrs. Parker said. "I've got lovely ideas for a simple fall garden."

"That sounds wonderful," Mom said, grinning. "Thank you."

Mom, Dad, and I stood to leave, so Paige could have a

minute alone with her parents before they headed home. "Here's a late housewarming gift, Sasha," Mrs. Parker said. She handed me a tiny potted plant.

"African violet," Paige whispered into my ear.

"A beautiful African violet," I repeated.

"It's one of the easiest potted plants to care for, so don't worry too much about it," Mrs. Parker said.

I held the plant carefully and hugged her with my free arm.

I watched over Mrs. Parker's shoulder as Heather and her parents got up from the table. Heather slunk out of the room behind them, looking herself like a wilted bloom.

20

SOMETIMES, EVEN BLOND SMURFS PLAY NICE. BUT ONLY SOMETIMES.

IT WAS HALLOWEEN NIGHT, AND CANTERWOOD Crest Academy was hosting a charity auction to benefit the Lucky Horse Rescue Center.

The spooky stable was full of skeletons, pumpkins on the counters, bats hanging from the ceiling, and candy corn stickers on the stall doors. Inside the arena, Mr. Conner stood with ten miniature horses from the local horse rescue.

The horses were under four feet tall at the withers. They'd all been rescued from neglectful or abusive homes.

The arena was bustling with students, miniature horses, and center directors. Callie and I had been assigned a black mare named India. One of the stable volunteers from Lucky Horse handed me India's lead line and we led her to crossties in the stable aisle. India stared shyly at the ground. Callie found the master list of available costumes and we read over the options.

"She would look adorable in the dragonfly costume," Callie said. "Or the bumblebee."

I took the list, smiling at the thought. "A clown isn't original enough and a princess is overdone." My eyes kept scanning. "How about a fairy?"

Callie snatched the list and looked over the costume pieces. "I love it!" she said. "You go get the costume and I'll start brushing her."

I ran to the arena before anyone could steal our costume. By the time I reached Callie, she had already brushed and buffed India into a shiny ebony. India blinked at us and let out a contented huff. My fingers ran over a jagged scar on her shoulder and I tried not to imagine where it had come from.

"I'll comb her mane flat and we can braid sparkly ribbons into it, okay?" I asked. "Then we can put on the costume." The costume bag contained pink wings and a shimmery girth to hold them.

"Definitely," she agreed as she combed the tail. "She's going to look beautiful!" While Callie finished the tail and tackled the braids, I brushed thick, glittery pink polish on India's hooves.

Charm watched us, peeking out from a couple of stalls down. He probably wanted a costume, too.

Callie fastened the elastic band around India and secured the wings on top. "We need to spray her with glitter."

I held the spray can away from India's face and put my finger on the trigger.

"What are you doing?" Heather asked, folding her arms across her chest. Her eyes scanned India's nearly finished costume.

"We're finishing our costume," Callie said. "Shouldn't you be finishing yours?" She took a soft purple brush and ran it across India's hindquarters. The horse stamped a hoof and tossed her head against the crossties. The longer we groomed her, the less shy she became.

"Julia and I would be working on Sahara's costume, but apparently the rules don't apply to you," Heather said slowly, as if she were speaking to children.

"Rules about what?" I asked.

"If you and Callie had been paying attention like the rest of us, you would have known there's a sign-up sheet for costumes. The fairy costume was taken because I signed up for it. You two, on the other hand, didn't sign up for a costume."

"Sorry." I shrugged. "Do you guys mind looking at other costumes? We're almost done."

Heather glared at me. "I *do* mind," she said. "Take it off and hand it over. I signed up for that costume—it's mine." She handed Callie a sheet of paper. I peered over Callie's shoulder and sure enough, Heather's name was printed neatly next to the fairy costume.

"Can't you guys just get a different costume?" Callie asked, putting down the hoof polish.

"Take it off and stop wasting my time," Heather said. She stepped in front of Callie and tapped the toe of her boot against the floor. "If you don't, I'll tell Mr. Conner."

While Heather blabbed away, India waited patiently for us to finish her costume.

"Like Mr. Conner will care about a stupid costume," Callie said.

Heather put a hand on her hip. "Give me the costume or I'm going to Mr. Conner. Your choice."

"No," Callie said, turning away from Heather.

I stepped up to Callie and whispered in her ear. "Let's just give her the costume. We'll get another one."

Callie stopped brushing India and stared at me. "Are you serious? We have twenty minutes until the auction!"

I reached for India's back and gently removed the wings. "Just give it to her."

"Are you on her side now?" Callie asked. "She's crazy! It's just a costume."

"She followed the rules," I said.

"Fine," Callie said. "But if we don't hurry, we'll be late and *none* of us will get credit for volunteering."

Heather stood by silently as Callie and I dismantled the costume and handed the pieces to her.

"You know, you're not as dumb as you look, Silver," Heather said brightly. She clutched the costume and skipped away. For a second, I fantasized about spraying her with the blue glitter. She'd look like a glittery blond Smurf.

Poor India was ready to get off the crossties and go for a walk.

"Give me the sheet and I'll go get whatever's left." Callie took the paper and went off to grab another costume. I swiped the polish-removing solution off the counter and wiped the paint off India's hooves. "You're not going to like this," Callie called to me.

"What?"

Callie forced a green blob of fabric into my hands.

"What is this?" I cried.

"It's a leprechaun."

"Like Lucky Charms-rainbow-and-pot-of-gold leprechaun?" I asked.

"Yep, that kind of leprechaun. We've got fifteen minutes to get her dressed and there were no other costumes, believe me."

We had no time to fight about the outfit. "Let's do it," I said, shaking the can and spraying India's tail.

Callie grabbed green hoof polish and repainted India's hooves a bright emerald green. We took the small green blanket with a silver four-leaf clover in the lower right corner and firmly attached the elastic straps around India's girth. I applied green clover stickers to India's neck and withers while Callie sprayed her mane with green glitter spray. For the final touch, we placed a large top hat on India's head and attached it to her halter. Callie and I stepped back and surveyed our handiwork. We had four minutes to spare.

"I love it," I said, standing shoulder to shoulder with Callie.

"I think I like it even better than the fairy costume," Callie said.

We unclipped India's crossties and led her forward.

"Wait." Callie placed a sparkly clover sticker on my cheek and I did the same to hers.

· · ·

Five of the horses sold at high prices to eager buyers interested in aiding the Lucky Horse Rescue Center. The students led the horses around in circles while the crowd exclaimed over the costumes. The pirate costume on a scrappy gelding drew loud applause and a mare in a motorcycle outfit got the crowd on their feet.

"Ladies and gents, may I now draw your attention to India," the auctioneer called. "This dainty black mare stands at seven hands high and is five years old. India was found starving and neglected at a local breeding farm but has bounced back as a lovely leprechaun! The bidding starts at one thousand."

"Twelve hundred," a man in the crowd called. India pricked her ears toward the crowd. *Too bad I couldn't bid on her. Charm would have loved a stable buddy.*

"I hear twelve hundred, do I hear thirteen hundred?" the announcer asked.

"Thirteen!" an elderly woman called.

"Fifteen hundred," the first man said, not waiting for the auctioneer and thrusting his paddle into the air.

After a few minutes of back and forth, India's bid rose to four thousand dollars!

"Oh, my God," I whispered to Callie.

"Unbelievable," she said. We squeezed hands and tried not to scream as we walked India around the ring. It felt like I had whiplash from turning my head every time someone in the audience made a bid.

"Four thousand going once," the announcer called. "Four thousand going twice. Sold for four thousand dollars to paddle number eighty-five!"

A white-haired woman who had made one of the first bids won. She hugged a man next to her and waved at Callie and me. Any worries I had about India getting a good family evaporated.

"Bye, India," I said. "You're going to a good home." Callie and I kissed India's muzzle and handed her off to one of the center's grooms. We skipped out of the ring and headed for the exit.

Callie draped her arm across my shoulders. "Can you believe that?" she asked.

"India's worth every cent," I said, grinning.

We hung by the door and watched as Julia and Heather stood in the center of the arena and led Sahara, clothed in the fairy costume, around in a circle.

Sahara's buckskin coat showed off the outfit, almost better than India had, and the bids stalled at three grand. Julia brought the horse to a halt and the crowd peered forward to see what was going on. Heather positioned herself in front of Sahara and stuck out her hand. "Shake," she commanded clearly. Sahara lifted her right front leg off the ground and placed her hoof in Heather's out-stretched hand.

The crowd burst into cheers. "Thirty-five hundred!" a man called from the crowd.

"I have thirty-five hundred, do I hear thirty-six?" The auctioneer took control of the excited crowd.

"Brilliant," I whispered to Callie.

Bids were flying so fast we could barely keep up.

"Sold!" The auctioneer banged his gavel. "Sold for four thousand to paddle number seven!"

Heather and Julia high-fived and rubbed Sahara's shoulders. A young girl, maybe six or seven, made her way into the arena. In one hand, she clutched a woman's hand and in the other, she held paddle number seven. Heather leaned over and whispered to the girl. The girl's black curls bounced as she stepped up to Sahara and patted her shoulder. While Julia held Sahara, Heather swooped up the girl and placed her on Sahara's back. The woman beamed and took the group's picture. I'd never seen Heather like this!

Heather and her little caravan headed our way. Sahara

pranced in her fairy costume and Callie and I parted so Heather could lead the horse through the doorway.

"Nice job," I said, expecting Heather and Julia to snip back.

"Thanks," Heather said. She grinned and looked back at the little girl playing with Sahara's mane.

Callie and I widened our eyes. "Let's go before she takes it back," Callie whispered.

We left the auction giggling. Maybe Heather knew how to be nice after all.

21

IT'S NOT *ABOUT* FRIENDSHIP

ON TUESDAY, ALGEBRA CLASS SEEMED TO drag on forever. At least my grade was a solid B plus in the class and I could spend more time on biology. School had *finally* started to feel a little easier. At least now I didn't feel like I had to study 24/7 to keep up with classes. And, hopefully, a couple of Bs on my report card would be okay with Mom and Dad.

When class finally ended, I headed back to the stable. Today, the riders were voting for the planner of the winter party.

"What's the winter party?" I had asked Callie earlier.

"Every fall, the team chooses a rider to throw a party," Callie said.

"How do we pick a winner?" I fished a piece of hay out of Charm's water bucket.

"Old school. We put our votes in a riding helmet. Last year, Heather won and she had a pink and white ball in the indoor arena. All of the girls dressed up in big, princess-y gowns. The arena looked like a Disney castle."

"That does sound fun," I admitted.

At that moment, I had known I wanted to plan the party. I was tired of being the girl I had been at Union Middle School where no one had known my name. The Canterwood Crest Sasha had to step up and take the reins.

Outside the math building, a crunchy, rust colored maple leaf floated in front of me and landed on the sidewalk. Barren trees dotted the campus. Winter was just around the corner. Cashmere sweaters replaced collared tees, wool skirts with tights replaced breezy cotton dresses. The dorms were toasty warm and I loved the feeling of cool air on my face. The outdoor pools were closed and now students spent more time at the campus movie theater or the bowling alley. Even Charm's coat was darkening from the lack of sunlight.

Soon, Mr. Conner would announce the student chosen to plan the winter party. Whoever won had only a couple of weeks to plan the event. Callie had said it was a Canterwood tradition that the winter party fell in November since students had too many activities, plus the winter holiday, in December.

I took a seat next to Callie. The Trio sat a few seats away. A smug-looking Julia leaned over Alison and whispered with Heather. Other riders filled the seats and chatted about who they thought would win. Mr. Conner entered and everyone looked at him expectantly.

"You're never this quiet when I have business to discuss," he said in a pretend-grumbling voice. "This year's planner of the winter riding event is . . ."

Callie and I sneaked a look at Heather and caught her staring back at me. Her eyes burned a hole in the side of my head as she glared and waited for Mr. Conner to call out the winner's name. Any shred of friendliness from the Halloween auction was long gone.

"Sasha Silver! Congratulations!" Mr. Conner said.

What? I looked to Callie, eyes wide.

An audible gasp came from Heather's side of the room.

"As I'm sure you know by now, the winter party has been a staple at Canterwood since the school began. Keep in mind that everyone will be expecting a grand scale event." Mr. Conner smiled at me. "You have two weeks to plan and I suggest you get started. When you have your plans, drop them by my office and I'll start ordering supplies."

"Oh, my God," I whispered. "Can you believe this?"

"Yes!" Callie cheered. "I can!"

I'd never planned a party! I tried to plan an anniversary dinner for my parents once and I forgot to put eggs in the cake mix, left the decorations at the checkout counter and forgot to invite them!

"I don't know," I said. "I'm freaking out here—what if I can't do this?"

"Calm down," Callie said. She took my arm and led me into the barn aisle. "I'll help you. We can do this together."

If I studied for midterms, packed for Thanksgiving break, wrote my film paper and took care of Charm, how would I be able to do the planning? Luckily, Mr. Conner had given us the week off from required practice so we could focus on studying instead of riding.

"Way to go, Sasha," Nicole said as she walked past me and clapped her hands. "You deserve it. I voted for you."

"Thanks, Nicole," I told her.

I still couldn't believe this. At Union, I hadn't even gone to any of the dances because I was always at Briar Creek. I was the stable girl and that was that. Here, smart kids liked me and actually voted for me to win! I hadn't been able to blend school and Briar Creek, but here, lots of people were riders *and* students, so no one teased me for being the horse girl.

Heather stomped in front of me. "Don't worry," she said, "We don't expect much from you. Just use whatever you had at your loser dances back home—lawn chairs and a cooler?"

"I've got to study," I told Callie, choosing to ignore Heather. "Call me later."

When I got into my dorm room, I immediately started on my English homework. Maybe the rules for writing a sonnet would seep into my brain if I put the book under my pillow tonight. But I couldn't focus.

Then an IM popped up.

GamerGuy: hey, sash. what r u doing?

My first IM conversation with Jacob!

SassySilver: hw. u?
GamerGuy: same. got a zillion papers 2 write b4 break.
SassySilver: me 2. and now i've got a party 2 plan.
GamerGuy: ?

SassySilver: @ the stables—the winter ball.

GamerGuy: cool. good luck.

Okay, here's where I *should* have asked him out. But I didn't.

SassySilver: thanx. c u ltr.

I logged out of IM and dialed Mom, in a pathetic attempt to avoid my homework.

"Hi, Mom," I said.

"Hey, hon. Dad and I were just talking about you! Only a two and a half more weeks until Thanksgiving break, huh?"

"I've got big news."

"Oh, really?" Mom asked.

"Yeah, it's really big." Making Mom squirm was kind of fun!

"Well, tell me!" Mom huffed.

"I am planning . . . ," Pause for dramatic effect. "The winter party for the riding team!" Silence. Not exactly the reaction I was after. "Mom?"

"Sasha, that's wonderful, but . . ." she said. "You're already doing so much."

"I want to do this. People voted for me!"

Mom's voice took a worried tone. "I just don't want you to overburden yourself."

"I won't."

"Won't this take away from your midterm studies?"

"No, Mom," I said impatiently. Why wasn't she more excited? "I'm studying right now."

"Okay," she said slowly. "Congratulations, Sasha—you know I'm proud of you."

When I got off the phone, I resumed my English home-work, which took over an hour to finish. Paige wasn't back yet, so I could at least outline party ideas before she got here. On the blank sheet of paper in front of me, I wrote *winter party*. Not nearly as confusing as sonnets. What was my party theme? That question needed an answer before I started my list. The rules said I was only in charge of food and decorations, but that was a big enough job. My mind was blank. And then I remembered: at Briar Creek, Charm's stall had always been my favorite thinking place. His stall here was twice as big.

I put my English book away and trudged back to the stable. The campus was unusually quiet. Everyone was probably in the library or holed up in a dorm studying for midterms. I gazed upward. Big, tumbling clouds filled the sky and a crisp breeze blew leaves from the sprawling oak and maple trees. If only campus was always this calm.

On my way to Charm's stall, I passed the indoor arena. Inside, Callie and Black Jack swept around the ring. Jack's black coat was slick with sweat. Since when did Callie practice without me? I had been studying my butt off and she was riding! Was school easy for everyone but me? I stepped inside the arena, careful not to startle Jack, and waved. Callie smiled and slowed Jack to a trot as they made their way over. "I thought you said you were studying," I said. "I didn't know you were going to practice."

Out of breath, she nodded and pushed hair out of her eyes. "Wasn't planning to, but I got bored with studying and felt like riding."

"I'll tack up Charm and practice with you," I said.

Callie hopped off Jack's back and loosened his girth. "I'm quitting. He's tired and I really need to get back to the dorm."

"We're still riding at four tomorrow, right?"

Callie led Jack away from me and out of the arena. "Of course—see you then!"

I took a seat at the side of the arena. Was Callie trying to get an edge over me? I got up, and almost collided with Heather. She had the batlike ability to sneak into any room without a sound.

"You're competition to her, Silver," Heather said. She was serious. She looked up from inspecting her pretty pink manicure and smirked at me, obviously enjoying my discomfort.

"Callie's my friend," I said. "She doesn't see me as competition." But the more I thought about it, the less sure I became.

Heather rolled her eyes, stepping closer. "This isn't *about* friendship. Everyone here wants to make that team. If you were smart, you'd be riding without her, too. Don't think I don't know that Julia sneaks off to ride without me."

"But Julia wouldn't stop being your friend if either of you didn't make the team." I knew that was true for Callie and me. Still, the more Heather said, the more paranoid I felt.

"Maybe not, but she doesn't see me as a friend when we ride. I'm just another person trying for the advanced team. Julia would be stupid if she didn't see me as competition. Same goes for Callie."

"You can be friends and still be competitive," I said. "It doesn't have to be like that." During my first trail ride with Callie, she had talked to me as if we'd been friends for years. But when she talked about the team and how she had ridden for the New England Saddle Club, for just a second, I knew she looked at me and wondered if I was someone to beat.

"Don't listen to me, then. But last year, Julia, Callie and I were the same. All on the same level and just as new to Mr. Conner. Julia practices without me all the time now."

I *had* noticed Julia's improvement every week. Her seat was stronger and her commands to Trix were enviably invisible.

"Callie and I would be happy if either of us made the team."

Heather planted her hands on her hips. "Really? If Callie makes the team and you don't, you won't care?"

"No," I argued. "I didn't say that. I'd care, I just—"

Heather took a step closer to me. "You wouldn't hate her? Or hate yourself for not working harder?"

I'd had enough. I headed for the door.

"She's here all the time, Sasha," Heather called after me. "She spent more time practicing today than you have all week."

The arena door banged shut behind me and I headed for Charm's stall. Jack's stall was empty—it looked like Callie was cooling him off somewhere. Deep down, I knew

Callie wasn't trying to best me, but Heather's warning rumbled around in my head. Charm and I weren't doing enough. Studying kept cutting into my riding time! Callie was lucky—school was easy for her. And Paige. And apparently Julia, Alison, and Nicole. Would school ever be easy again?

"C'mon Charm," I said to him as he looked up at me from the hay net. Hay stuck out the corners of his mouth. "It's time to work."

Two hours later, it was after six, and I'd missed dinner. Charm and I, sweaty and sore, soared over two double oxers. Livvie had grudgingly agreed to let me practice for a few hours, as long as I had promised to relax the rest of the night. My phone vibrated in my pocket and Charm slowed to a walk so I could look at my caller ID.

"Where are you?" Callie asked.

"Eating with Paige," I told her. "I'd invite you, but we're having our dorm meeting." Guilt settled in my stomach. I hadn't meant to lie. We chatted for a minute before hanging up. I clicked the phone shut and placed it back in my pocket. Charm and I had another hour before we would stop.

It was time to get serious.

22

THE S.I.N.G. TECHNIQUE IS GOOD FOR LOTS OF THINGS. . . .

THE LIGHTS IN THE THEATER CAME ON AS THE credits rolled.

"Did you like it?" Jacob asked. Mr. Ramirez wanted to show us a true blockbuster film, so he'd picked one of the biggest-grossing movies in history—*Jurassic Park*.

"I loved it," I said. "But I was scared most of the time!"

"Even though there was a roomful of people?" Jacob asked.

"Sorry, but Mr. Ramirez couldn't stop a T-Rex from snatching us out of a Jeep," I said.

"True," he conceded.

"I was getting ready to use my S.I.N.G. technique," I said.

"What is the S.I.N.G. technique?"

"S.I.N.G. Solar plexus, instep, nose, and groin." I mimed punching and kicking the imaginary dinosaur.

Jacob laughed.

"Don't make me use it on you," I teased.

Jacob held up his hands in a mock okay-okay-I'm-backing-off gesture.

We gathered our bags and headed out.

"We're watching *The King and I* next week, right?" I asked.

"I think so," Jacob said.

Okay, just ask him. Yoga-breath time. In, out. Iiiiiiin, ouuuuut.

"The dancing scenes look cool," I said. "Lots of parties. And dancing . . ." I trailed off. I couldn't do it. The words to ask Jacob to the dance just wouldn't come out. I stopped myself from turning and grabbing my plum lip gloss out of my bag.

Jacob shook his head. "I'm an awful dancer."

"Me, too," I said.

Jacob shifted his film textbook from one arm to the next. "Hey, Sasha," he said.

"You want me to teach you the S.I.N.G. technique, don't you?" I asked.

He laughed. "You're funny." He glanced down at his sneakers before looking back up at me. "I'm going to the library to study."

I nodded, unsure what he wanted me to say. "Have fun," I said.

"Do you want to come?" he asked. "I could help you with bio and you could help me with English."

Was this a date? I wanted to call Paige for advice. But Jacob smiled and I felt less nervous.

"Cool," I said. "Let's go!"

Forty-five minutes later, we were elbow-deep in textbooks. Ms. Langford, the librarian, kept swooping in and eyeing us suspiciously. Whenever our voices rose above an exaggerated whisper, she looked daggers at us.

In the last couple of months, I'd spend a lot of time in the library, but, as with the rest of campus, I never got used to how beautiful it was. There was polished, dark mahogany wood everywhere; tiny gold reading lamps with forest green shades dotted every table, casting a cozy yellow glow over everything. The book collection was a thousand times bigger than the one at Union, and Canterwood's library, unlike Union's, was never empty.

"So," I said, leaning across the table toward Jacob.

"Do you get the symbolism in *The Red Badge of Courage*?"

"Thanks to you," he said. "Do you understand the difference between osmosis and diffusion?"

"I do," I said, closing my book. "And I think my brain is stuffed. Are midterms always like this?" I asked. I couldn't remember ever studying this hard before.

"They're worse than last year, that's for sure. I'm kind of wishing I was back in sixth grade right now!"

I nodded back at him, but I wasn't wishing for sixth grade at all. Sixth grade had meant squirming through classes while really wanting to be in the stables and friends who hadn't understood why I'd rather ride horses instead of shouting "Go team!" during pep rallies.

Canterwood was different. It taught me that I could have both—riding and school—and that, as long as I was following my dreams of making the advanced team *and* doing well in classes, that's all that really mattered.

"So that was solar plexus, instep, nose, and what?" Jacob chided.

"Groin," I said.

"I wonder if that will be on your bio test?" he asked.

"I wonder if you should write your English paper," I laughed.

23

MR. CONNER'S NOT-SO-SECRET HIDING SPOT

MIDTERMS CAME WITH A FURY.

And when Paige and I weren't studying, we were party planning. We barricaded ourselves in our dorm for days. We had piles of notebooks, papers, flashcards, and books. Ms. Peterson uploaded a couple of helpful online video tutorials, all of which I watched at least twice.

Paige had baked two dozen cappuccino fudge brownies in the communal kitchen and I had raided the vending machines for sodas and study snacks. Being inside wasn't too bad, since there was an unexpected cold front that had frozen over the entire campus. The horses were stuck inside—just like the riders.

I felt torn between the stable and studying. When I rode Charm, I felt like I should be back here. But when

I started to study, guilt crept over me because I wasn't practicing. I had ridden when I could with Callie, but had little time to practice on my own. Maybe Callie was riding while I was pouring over Spanish verbs.

Now, Paige and I were dissecting the Heather conversation for the thousandth time.

"Do you really believe Heather, though?" Paige asked. "I mean, it's *Heather*. You know she's a liar."

"I know, but Callie *was* practicing without me," I said, putting down my pink highlighter. "I'm probably way behind everyone on practice time."

Paige shook her head. "I doubt it. I'd think you'd notice if your riding wasn't up to par."

"I never thought there was a rivalry with Callie and me, but maybe I'm wrong," I said.

Paige closed her worn history textbook and headed for the minifridge. "I wouldn't worry about it. Even if she does practice without you sometimes, so what? I don't think it's that she's trying to outdo you."

"I really hope not."

"Why don't you stop wondering and just call her?" Paige handed me my phone. "Ask her and get it out in the open."

Paige was right. I picked up the phone before I could chicken out.

"I'm so glad you called," Callie said when she answered. "Heather just tripped in the common room and dumped a huge frozen hot chocolate all over Alison! It was awesome."

"Oh," I replied flatly.

"Are you okay?" Callie asked. "I thought you'd love that!"

"What are you doing this afternoon?" I asked her.

"Riding." Her tone sounded like it should be obvious.

"So, you're practicing without me."

"What are you talking about?" Callie asked.

"You just said you were riding," I said. Heather had been right all along.

"Yeah, I'm riding with you!" Callie said. "Didn't you see the note on your door?"

I yanked the door open and glanced up and down. No note. Just our whiteboard with the pink daisy Paige had drawn last night. "I don't see anything."

"It was a blue star sticky note," Callie said. "I was passing by Winchester, so I left you a note asking if you wanted to ride with me today."

I looked up and down the hallway in case it had fallen on the floor. "There's nothing here," I said.

"You're my friend," Callie said, sounding hurt. "You don't think I'm lying . . . do you?"

I didn't say anything for a minute.

"You don't want to come out and ride with me?" Callie asked.

"No, I do. I'll meet you in a couple of hours," I said, still unsure, and hung up.

"She swears she left a note," I said to Paige.

"I never saw it," she said. "But maybe it fell off and someone threw it away."

There was no sign of the note, but no time to dwell on it, either. I had to fit in some more party-planning time before our ride. Paige made hot chocolate for us, and I grabbed two boxes of raisins from the cabinet. Last night, when Paige and I had been chatting until we had fallen asleep, we'd decided on a blue, white, and silver icy winter theme. I pulled out my checklist. Wow—it looked like a lot of things were already checked off! I scanned the list for what was left to do.

> *distribute fliers*
> *ask Mr. Conner to buy more glitter*
> *check on cider delivery*
> *food: chips, dip, packaged cupcakes*
> *sleighs arrived yet?*

The sleighs. Mr. Conner had agreed to order them after I had showed him the weather station's prediction that we'd get an early snow. November didn't come with many snow days, but everyone had their fingers crossed that we'd be enjoying sleigh rides on party night. Luckily, the temperature had been hovering just above thirty degrees for the past couple of days.

I switched on my computer and printed. I read it aloud to Paige. "'What: Winter Wonderland Party for the riding team. When: the Saturday before Thanksgiving break at seven p.m. Where: the Canterwood Equestrian indoor arena. Come dressed in your best and be ready for a night of snow, horses, and fun!'"

"Sounds great to me," Paige said. "When you make copies, save me some and I'll hang them up."

"Great idea—thanks!"

"How's the rest of the list coming?" she asked, holding out her hand.

I handed it over to her.

"*Packaged* cupcakes?" she shrieked. "*Chips and dip*?!"

"No good?" I asked her.

Paige wrinkled her nose.

"Ugh—you're right," I sighed. "It's totally lame. I just—" Then inspiration hit. Paige Parker was *the* girl for the job.

"What?" Paige asked. "You have a weird look on your face."

"Are you interested in planning the menu for the winter party?" I asked her.

"Are you kidding?" Paige squealed. "Of course!"

"Are you sure you have time?" I asked her. "The party is less than two weeks away."

"It'll be just like The Food Network," she said. "I'll have a short time to prep for a big bash. This is great practice for the next casting call! I'll start planning the list right now. What do you think about snowflake sugar cookies with royal icing?"

"Perfect!" I said.

"And," Paige continued, "according to Martha Stewart's *Three Thousand Treats for Any Party,* we've got to have homemade ice cream, a hot drink, and some type of wheat crackers with cheese."

With most of my list taken care of, I headed for the stables. No one was roaming campus, since studying seemed to be this week's top priority.

The indoor arena was locked up until the party started in a few days, to encourage students to spend their time studying rather than riding. Mr. Conner had left me the key so I could check on my decorations and store other supplies for the party, so I decided to take inventory before I met Callie.

My paddock boots thumped on the concrete on my way to Mr. Conner's office. I swiped the arena key from under his coffee pot (his idea for a secret key location).

When I got closer to the arena, I saw a light peeking out from under the arena door. Someone was inside! Either Mr. Conner was still around or someone else knew about Mr. Conner's secret hiding spot.

I pulled the door open.

Black Jack cantered around the arena, his royal blue leg wraps flashing, and Callie guided him around the banquet tables and decoration boxes. If she got caught riding in the supposed-to-be-locked arena, she'd be on serious probation. What was she thinking?

"Callie!" I yelled.

Callie's head snapped around as she looked at me. She slowed Jack from a posting trot to a walk.

"Hey!" Callie exclaimed with a smile.

"You're not supposed to be in here!" I said. "Mr. Conner would freak if he found out. How'd you get in, anyway?"

"Mr. Conner has been hiding keys under that coffee pot for months," Callie said, laughing.

"But we're not supposed to ride in here," I said. "I thought we were going to practice in the outer aisles."

Callie shook her head. "We'll only be here for half an hour. Besides, we need the bigger space."

"Okay," I grudgingly agreed. "Be right back." I'd worry about the party after our ride. And anyway, wasn't Mr. Conner the one who kept telling us to practice? He knew midterms were upon us and he'd cut back our riding schedules. But he also kept saying it was up to us to practice when we could.

Still, I couldn't help but wonder why Callie had gotten here so much earlier than we were supposed to meet. And I wanted to believe her about the note, but she had been acting pretty strange lately. Was she just as stressed as I was or . . . was my best friend lying to me?

24

GOTTA GET A GOOD GRADE

PAIGE AND I WALKED OUT OF THE MATH building and adjusted our backpacks on our shoulders. "That was almost too easy," Paige said. "Aced it for sure."

"I'm hoping for at least a B plus in algebra," I said. "The last set of equations tripped me up."

"Did Callie do okay?" Paige asked.

"I'm sure she did fine," I said. Things had been okay between Callie and me lately, almost like normal again, but I still wondered about that note. "But I walked by Heather's math class. She wasn't even writing anything. She looked like she wanted to cry."

"You'd think her parents would understand that they're putting way too much pressure on her," Paige said.

"If she fails, she won't be able to ride," I said. "It's not just her parents."

Paige linked arms with me. "I know if she had asked you for help, you would have helped her."

We walked up to the science building. Bio. Breathe in, breathe out. In, out. In, out. Okay, this wasn't helping. I felt less like I was "centering" myself and more like I was about to hyperventilate. Paige let go of my arm. "Good luck," she said. "It's your last midterm!"

"Yeah, but this it's the hardest one," I grumbled.

"You'll do fine," Paige assured me. "See you in the dorm."

Every subject was easy for Paige. I envied her. Sure, she studied hard, but it felt like I had to study twice as hard just to keep up with her.

I stood outside room 207 and waited. Parts of the cell, kingdoms, and anatomy ran through my brain. Were there four stages of mitosis or five?

"Sasha?"

I turned and saw Jacob.

"Science midterm?" I asked, cheered up momentarily.

He nodded and adjusted his black messenger bag with a tiny pirate skull and crossbones sticker on it. "Just finished. You?"

I looked toward room 207. "Any second now."

Jacob smiled. "I know you'll do great."

People started streaming out of the room. "I better go in and get a seat."

Jacob looked like he wanted to say something. "Sasha?"

"Yeah?" I asked.

He hesitated. "Nothing," he said. "Good luck."

I slid into my seat and read my notes while Ms. Peterson shuffled some papers on her desk. The rest of the class, including Alison and Julia, filed in and took their seats.

Julia turned to hang her backpack off the back of her chair. Our eyes met, but she turned around without saying anything.

I put away my books and then Julia craned her head back around. "Good luck," she said.

Alison nudged her. "Um, hello?" she said.

"You, too," I said to Julia.

"All right, class," Ms. Peterson said. "Quiet. This test is worth twenty-five percent of your grade, so I hope you're prepared."

25

THE ONLY ONES
SLEEPING

THE DAYS AFTER MIDTERMS FLEW BY IN A flurry of practice for testing and party planning. I'd left Ms. Peterson's biology midterm feeling as though I'd done well. The endless hours of studying *had* to pay off. We wouldn't get our midterm grades until after we came back from break, so Paige had convinced me not to worry about them.

Instead, we focused on the party! Paige had scrapped about a dozen possible menus before narrowing it down to a select few choices.

It was time for my last riding lesson before Saturday's testing—tomorrow! After I tacked up Charm, we joined Callie, Nicole, and the Trio in the indoor arena.

"How does everyone feel about testing tomorrow?" Mr. Conner asked.

"Terrified," Callie said, looking like she was only half joking.

"I'm not *that* tough, am I?" Mr. Conner grinned. "Let's relax and run through a few exercises. I want you to sleep well tonight and feel ready for tomorrow. Let's start with a walk." Charm was excited to be practicing, I could tell.

"Kick your feet out of the stirrups and do a sitting trot," Mr. Conner directed.

Charm moved into a trot and I tried not to bounce on his back. We made a couple of circuits around the arena.

"Slow to a walk, put your feet back in the stirrups and stand," Mr. Conner called.

I grabbed Charm's stubby mane to steady myself and stood in the stirrups as we walked.

Nicole lost her balance and plopped into the saddle. She shook her head and stood back up.

Mr. Conner put us through a few more exercises and then waved us over. "Let's run through how tomorrow's going to work," he said.

All eyes rested on him.

"The intermediate team, as you're well aware, tests tomorrow," he said. "The five of you and thirteen riders from the other intermediate groups are testing. I'll pass around this clipboard in a second and you can sign up for time slots."

Mr. Conner handed out the clipboard and Callie and I signed our names next to the two and three o'clock slots.

"You're all currently riding on a three point five level," Mr. Conner continued. "You need to reach a four to make the advanced team. No one will be in the arena except for you and me during your test. Any questions?"

No one had any.

"Charm and Jack are going to be the only ones sleeping tonight," I said to Callie.

26

NOT EVEN LUCK
WILL HELP YOU NOW

CALLIE WAS GROOMING JACK IN THE CROSSTIES.
Today was *the* day. Testing day for the advanced team.

"Have you ever tested before?" I asked her.

"I tested when I rode for the New England Saddle
Club," Callie said. "But I came here before testing for
their advanced team. Was there testing at your stable?"

I circled the rubber currycomb over Charm's already
clean coat. He snorted a warning when I curried the
same spot for too long. I switched to a soft brush and
swept any invisible specks of dust off his back. "No, my
stable didn't have testing. We rode in levels but nothing
like this." Charm snorted. The days of dozing in the
pasture were long gone. "You've been great, boy," I said,
rubbing his back.

Callie brought me back to reality. "I've got to go warm up, but you're going to do great. I know you'll make it."

"Thanks," I said. I could tell she'd meant it.

I smoothed the saddle pad onto Charm's back and tried not to plop the heavy English saddle on top of it. "Ready for this, boy?" I asked. Charm nodded and tugged on the crossties. "This is it. We have to do this right."

Saddling Charm never got any easier, no matter how many two-pound weights I lifted. When I tightened the girth, I could have sworn there was a girth cinched around my own stomach.

"You okay?" I asked Charm. He bobbed his head and nudged me forward.

Inside the arena, Mr. Conner and Heather talked in low tones while Aristocrat tugged on the reins. I mounted Charm and started to warm up while Heather finished. She led Aristocrat in front of us before she left.

"Good luck, Silver," she said. "I'd say 'you'll need it,' but not even luck will help you now. You don't have a chance."

"Then you should have nothing to worry about," I said, squeezing my heels against Charm's side. I sat deep in the saddle, passing Heather and Aristocrat.

It was time to focus.

Charm trotted over to the banquet table where Mr. Conner was still writing on Heather's chart. He had stacked all of the decorations under the table and had slid the rest of the boxes along the wall.

I waited for him to finish. Charm shifted his weight and stretched his neck. Mr. Conner finally stopped scribbling and looked up at me. He gave me a smile. "Ready, Sasha?"

"I'm ready."

He pulled out my chart and poised his pen. "It's going to be simple. You'll follow all of my commands until I tell you to stop. When I give you a new direction, begin that task immediately. Understand?"

"Got it." I grasped the reins and straightened. Charm was in spectacular condition—bathed, braided, and brushed. If I rode him correctly, we'd do just fine. Charm calmed down as I rubbed my hands along his neck.

"Let's start with something easy," Mr. Conner called. "Do a posting trot."

I squeezed Charm's sides until he trotted. We made sweeping circles around the arena—posting was second nature by now. I stared between the tips of Charm's ears. I rose and fell with his inside shoulder. His hooves thudded evenly across the arena dirt. He trotted easily—I knew we'd nailed the first task. "Great job, boy," I whispered.

"Slow canter," Mr. Conner called.

I tapped my boots against Charm's sides and he eased into a rocking canter. I sat motionless, keeping my butt glued to the seat. We swept around the arena.

"Flying lead change across the diagonal," Mr. Conner announced.

My stomach dropped.

I had only been doing flying changes since the summer. The move was one of the trickiest tasks on horseback. They had to be done just right. I had only performed a few and most of them had been on Kim's much more experienced Danish Warmblood. While cantering, I had to signal Charm to switch lead hooves. All four of his legs were supposed to leave the ground for a split second as we hit the center point of the arena. Most riders couldn't correctly command the horse to do flying changes—the horse would canter though the diagonal and end up on the wrong lead.

I wondered if Heather had been able to do the flying change.

"Okay, boy. We can do this," I said. We headed for the far end of the arena. Charm cantered toward the center. When we reached the middle, I shifted my weight and pulled slightly back on the reins. I moved my outside leg behind the girth and put my other leg just at the girth. I tried to reposition Charm with the reins, but he pulled against my fingers and awkwardly cantered on the wrong lead until I slowed him to a trot. I tried not to look over at Mr. Conner. "Please, Charm," I whispered to him. "Work with me here!" One of his ears swiveled back to my voice.

Charm quickened his pace. We headed to an imaginary X in the arena's center and we crossed over the middle. I asked him again for the flying lead change. Without hesitation, he switched leads and for a nanosecond, he suspended in the air. "Yes!" I whispered. "Yay, boy!"

Mr. Conner didn't tell us to stop, so I turned Charm around and pointed him to the middle of the area. We cantered to the center and he did another flying change without a hitch.

"Take a break while I set up a few jumps," Mr. Conner called from the sidelines.

I pulled Charm into a walk and he mouthed the bit. Foam specks flew from his mouth and landed on his chest and legs. "You're doing great," I said to Charm. "Maybe Paige and I will bake you an apple pie when we're done." Charm walked in slow circles. I let the knotted reins rest against his neck while I reached my hands to the sky in a stretch.

Mr. Conner set up four jumps consisting of red and

white plastic rails, each increasing in height up to about three feet high. He waved me over, clipboard still in hand. "You're going to jump the course twice: once clockwise and once counterclockwise. If you hit a rail, keep going. I'm going to take notes on your form and approach, as well as Charm's behavior. After this, you can cool him down and you're free to go."

Charm tugged the reins and scratched his knee with his teeth. Walking in circles bored him when he saw jumps up ahead.

Eight rails. That's all that stood between the advanced team and me.

"Ready?" I asked Charm.

He bobbed his head.

"Let's go."

Charm thudded over the last jump in the clockwise round. I turned him sharply to take the jumps counterclockwise. We didn't even come close to touching a rail in the first round. My legs had begun to shake from fatigue and white froth formed at the front corners of Charm's wool saddle pad. Charm was getting tired, but he managed to pop over each jump with the same power.

I pointed him toward the first jump and he took it like a pro. One down, three to go. The second jump didn't faze Charm either. He tucked his legs neatly as he sailed over the third rail. Charm took an extra circle before we headed for the final jump. I was barely even aware that Mr. Conner was in the ring. We were strides away from finishing when a light flashed. The door swung open and slammed against the arena wall.

"Mr. Conner!" a shrill voice called. Heather strode into the arena and headed right for Mr. Conner.

Charm shied violently and almost tripped as he crab-stepped the last jump. My foot popped out of the right stirrup as I started to fall off Charm's left side. I was not going to fall off in front of Heather and Mr. Conner!

"Easy, easy!" I said. My thighs hugged the saddle and I pulled myself upright. I grabbed his short mane and settled myself back in the saddle. Charm was anxious. He started to gallop to the final rail, his ears swept back in fear. His gait increased with every step and he acted like he didn't see the jump in front of us. I couldn't let him crash into the rail! *Charm, slow down!* I stood in the stirrups and used a pulley rein to circle him just before the jump.

I glanced over and saw Heather hurrying over to Mr. Conner.

"I am *so* sorry—the door got away from me! I was just coming to tell you that the grain delivery is here."

Mr. Conner glared at Heather and called out to me, "Sasha! Are you okay?"

"Fine," I called back, my hands shaking so hard they could barely grip the reins. Charm could have tripped or hit the jump. I bent over Charm's left shoulder and noticed his leg wrap was starting to come undone. "Heather?" I called. "Would you fix Charm's wrap for me?"

"Of course, Sasha." Heather walked over to Charm and slid her hand down his leg to tighten his leg wrap. Charm tried to walk off when he saw Heather coming, but I held him still.

"I know you did that on purpose," I whispered, keeping an eye on Mr. Conner.

Heather continued to tuck the stretchy fabric into the wrap as she spoke. "Oh, please, it was an accident."

"Stay away from me and Charm," I said.

Heather gave Charm's shoulder a firm pat and clasped my boot-clad ankle. "That's the smartest thing you've said all day."

Mr. Conner finished scribbling on my chart and, when he looked up at us, Heather's face morphed into an angelic smile.

"Be more careful next time, Heather," Mr. Conner said. "Sasha, thank you. You can go walk Charm until he's cool."

I dismounted and tugged on Charm's reins to get him away from Heather. Mr. Conner didn't even let me do the course again.

We'd failed.

27

A WELL-DESERVED WALK

THE NEXT DAY, PAIGE SAT ON THE EDGE OF my bed and pulled down my comforter.

"Sasha?" she said. I burrowed deeper into my flannel sheets. "You have to get up sometime."

"I didn't make the team," I grumbled, trying to cover my head with my bedspread. "I'm not getting out of bed."

"You don't know that," Paige said. "Besides, Mr. Conner knows what happened."

"I should have said something," I said.

"You were the better person by not ratting her out."

I didn't say anything. Paige deserved one of those cheesy "world's best roomie" mugs.

"Sash, it's Sunday afternoon. You haven't seen Charm since yesterday. Get up, get dressed and go see him."

"Fine," I said.

"You better not be here when I get back," Paige said, grabbing her messenger bag and heading out the door.

How could I face Charm? If I had been paying more attention to the arena instead of focusing so much on the jump, maybe he wouldn't have bolted. He had been counting on me to guide him and I'd failed.

My phone rang and I answered it.

"How'd you do?" Kim asked excitedly.

I told her the whole story.

"Sasha," Kim said. "Mr. Conner knows what competition is like! He knew exactly what Heather was doing. If, and it's an unlikely if, you don't make the team, it's because you and Charm aren't ready. Not because of Heather. You gave your best ride and that's all you could do."

"Charm did great," I said, thinking back to how he had roared over the jumps. "He listened to all of my commands. He was really centered."

"Then think about that and be happy with your ride! Charm did everything you asked," she said. "That's the best kind of ride!"

My eyes filled with tears—not because I worried about not making it, but because while I sulked in bed, Charm was all alone in the stable. "I've gotta go."

I tossed on a pair of yesterday's jeans and left for the stables. There was no excuse for leaving Charm alone for an entire day.

The stable was quiet when I arrived. "Hey," I said, peering inside. Charm had his head down by his water bucket. He turned his head toward my voice. "You okay?" Both ears pricked forward. His big brown eyes locked on mine. "I'm coming in." Charm stepped back and made a tiny space for me to squeeze between him and the door.

Once inside, I put my arms around his neck and hugged him. I stroked his mohawk mane. "I never should have run out on you after testing. You did great yesterday. I should have at least brushed you and made sure you were okay."

Charm stamped his hoof.

"I'm going to groom you, like I should have done yesterday, and then we'll go for a walk." Charm bobbed his head. Smart horse.

I took the side of Charm's halter and led him to the crossties. He stood still in the aisle while I clipped the ropes to his halter rings. I grabbed his tack box and started on his forelock. His mane was too short to be combed, so I tackled a couple of tangles in his long tail. Using one of his no-tears wipes, I wiped off his muzzle and eye area. The stiff dandy brush took the tough bits of dirt out of his coat and I finished by running a soft brush over his barrel, legs and neck. Next, I pried dirt out of his hooves.

In the time since I had started grooming Charm, my anger and sadness had begun to slip away. He had that effect on me.

I unclipped him from the crossties. We headed down the aisle.

Nicole had her gelding, Wish, on a lead line. Wish stretched his muzzle out to Charm.

"We're going for a walk," I said to Nicole. "Want to come?"

"We'd love to," she said.

Our horses' hooves clip-clopped down the aisle as we led them outside for a well-deserved walk.

28

ONE BIG QUESTION AND A LITTLE PARTY PLANNING

PAIGE MADE ME HELP HER WITH THE FOOD for the party to keep my mind off testing. I wouldn't care if I didn't see another cupcake for the rest of my life! It was only Tuesday, but Paige was in full-out baking mode.

And this afternoon, I was going to the stables to decorate for Saturday's party.

Before I left my dorm, I logged in to IM and sighed with relief when I saw *GamerGuy*'s icon was dark. If Jacob had been online, I might have been too nervous to ask what I wanted to ask.

SassySilver: hey, jacob. the stable party is on sat. if u having nothing planned and u want to come, it might be fun. let me know! ttyl.

I logged out before he could get online and ran on nervous energy all the way to the stable.

Nicole and Callie had asked if they could help decorate, so I'd organized a decorating party at four.

"Hey, where's the party?" Callie asked.

"We *have* to outdo Heather," Nicole said, pulling off her purple scarf.

I laughed, whipping out my heavily scribbled-on to-do list.

I began divvying up the duties. "Nicole, could you hang lights? You're the tallest. Callie, can you do the streamers? I'll start setting up the banquet tables."

While Callie and Nicole went off to tackle their respective tasks, I grabbed a box of snowflake window clings and started sticking the blue and white snowflakes to the windows.

Three hours later, it was almost seven and everyone was still going strong.

"Do you like the tree?" Nicole asked, nodding to the artificial tree she had set up.

"Perfect," I said. Callie unfolded a stepladder and held it so that Nicole could climb up and hang popcorn, beads, and sparkly glass balls on the tree.

Nicole and I had decorated the outside of the arena

with clear twinkly lights. They looked amazing.

I started spraying faux snow around the arena windows since the forecast was still officially undecided for Saturday. When I was done, I covered the banquet tables with crystal-like confetti and white-frosted candles. The table glittered and the confetti sparkled in the light.

"It's was just a dusty arena a few hours ago," Callie said. "Now it's a party palace!"

"Are we outdoing Heather yet?" Nicole asked.

"By far," Callie said, grinning.

But, looking around at my friends and the beautiful Winter Wonderland we'd created together, I realized I wasn't even thinking about Heather. It was a good feeling.

29

LISTEN TO
OTHER PEOPLE'S
CONVERSATIONS MUCH?

IT WAS TOO EARLY ON A WEDNESDAY MORNING when my phone jolted me awake.

"What?" I grumbled.

"Grumpy, grumpy!" Mom said in that singsong voice that drove me crazy.

"I'm not grumpy. Just tired," I said, groaning.

"I'm excited you're coming home this weekend, hon."

"Me too," I told her. I realized that over the past couple of days, I hadn't even thought of home—or Mom and Dad—once! If someone had told me two months ago I'd be at boarding school and not missing home like crazy, I'd have thought they were insane.

"I just wanted to remind you to bring your laundry home," Mom said.

"Um, okay," I said, looking guiltily at the heap of dirty clothes spilling out of my hamper.

"Are you all set for the dance?" she asked.

I smiled, thinking about how much my friends had helped me with all the planning. "It's going to be really fun, I think," I told her.

"Well, have fun, sweetie. We'll see you soon."

I pulled myself out of bed. There was a ton of packing to be done before Sunday. But first, I logged onto my IM. Immediately, a message popped up.

GamerGuy: hey! that sounds like fun. i'll b there if my parents don't come early 2 pick me up. c ya ltr. ☺

A smiley face!

"Yes!" I screamed, causing Paige to open one eye and sit up in bed.

"That better be something really, really good," she said, rubbing her eyes.

"Jacob wants to come to the party!" I said, hopping up and down.

"Sasha!" Paige jumped out of bed and read the IM. "Oh, my God! He's totally in love with you. I know it."

I laughed. "Let's see if he shows up to the dance first."

After a quick shower, I slipped into a sweater and flared jeans on loan from Paige and headed to Livvie's office.

"What's up?" Livvie asked. She motioned for me to sit on her desk chair.

"I wanted to let you know that my parents will be here by five on Sunday."

"Thanks," Livvie said, marking the time off on her clipboard. "Do you feel ready to go home?"

"It feels kind of strange," I admitted. "But I'm looking forward to sleeping in my own bed again."

"Do you think you'll visit your old stable?" Livvie asked.

Briar Creek. With all that had been going on, it hadn't even crossed my mind. "I don't know," I said, thinking of B.C.'s new rider—Lauren.

Livvie seemed to know what I was thinking. "It's okay to go back. I bet your old instructor would love to see you."

"Maybe," I said, realizing that was probably true.

Livvie checked her watch. "You better get to English."

As I headed for Mr. Davidson's class, I spotted Julia and Alison up ahead on a picnic bench.

"She thinks her dad's going to make her leave because of her grades," I heard Julia say. "She said she may not even be here for—" Julia stopped and turned around. "Um, can we help you?" she asked me.

"Yeah, hello! Listen to other people's conversations much?" Alison added.

"Whatever," I said, walking away. But I was too distracted to be mad at their snarks. Maybe they weren't even talking about Heather. Canterwood classes were notoriously tough—it could have been any girl they were talking about.

But if Mr. Fox did make Heather leave, he was more awful than I thought. Even Heather didn't deserve to be yanked out of her home.

I slid into my seat next to Callie. Mr. Davidson was bent over his desk.

"We're getting test grades back," Callie whispered.

Mr. Davidson started calling out names and passing back papers. "Jen. Erika. Cole. Sasha." He handed me my paper. It was folded over. I closed my eyes and pictured the letter A.

I let the paper unfold and opened my eyes.

A.

I did it!

Callie got her paper and checked it. She smiled and slid it off the corner of her desk so I could see. B+.

Maybe I was finally getting used to Canterwood classes after all.

30

BITTERSWEET
ALMOST-VICTORY

"HEATHER'S WORSE THAN EVER!" I SAID TO
Callie in the tack room later that afternoon.

We were sorting laundry for Charm and Jack. Leg
wraps, sweat sheets, and saddle pads needed to be washed
before we went home on Sunday.

"I thought she'd be in a good mood because she's so
sure she made the team, but she's being awful," I said.
"But I guess she would be, if her dad's threatening to
make her leave."

Yesterday, she had blocked the aisle with Aristocrat and
had refused to let anyone go around her. She made such a
fuss that anyone who needed to get out of the stable went
around the back and walked through the frozen mud. No
one had dared argue with her.

"She does seem nastier," Callie agreed. "Maybe her dad said she's definitely going."

"I don't know," I said, tossing two of Charm's red leg wraps into the laundry pile. I had told Callie earlier about what I'd overheard. "Maybe you can find out something in Orchard."

Callie nodded. "I'll ask around when I go back to my room." She aimed for the laundry pile and Jack's blue leg wrap sailed through the air and hit me on the knee.

"Ow!" I yelped, feigning pain from the neoprene wrap. "Now I'll have a limp."

Callie laughed and chucked another wrap at me. "Take that!"

I ducked behind the saddle racks and tossed a balled-up saddle cover at her.

"Truce! Truce!" Callie squealed, waving one of Jack's white neck sweats. She collapsed on the floor and laughed. I flopped down beside her on a hay bale and we laughed until our sides were sore.

I was settled into bed, watching an episode of *Southampton Socialites,* when my phone rang. Paige was flipping through *Hot Hairstyles* trying to decide if she needed bangs. My vote was no, but she wasn't convinced.

"You will *not* believe this!" Callie half-shouted into the phone. "I know what's going on with Heather!"

I pushed the speakerphone button and put my ear close to the phone. "Paige is listening, too."

"I heard that Heather's parents are transferring her out of Canterwood for *sure*," Callie said.

"No," I said, not really believing it. "Really?"

"Heather and Aristocrat leave this weekend," Callie confirmed. "I heard it from this girl in my dorm who overheard Alison and Julia talking about it. She won't even be at the team announcements."

"That's awful," Paige said.

"I feel bad," I said. "Heather must have been devastated when she found out."

Callie chewed into the phone as she spoke. "I hate to be the one to say it, but our chances at making the advanced team just drastically improved," she said.

I was silent, but Callie was right. Heather had been our biggest competition. We still weren't guaranteed spots, but our future at Canterwood suddenly looked brighter.

I knew I should have felt happier. If victory was closer than ever, why did it feel so bittersweet?

31

YOU DON'T SUCK

CHARM MUST HAVE JUST TAKEN A DRINK because when he came to greet me, bits of hay and sticky grain were stuck to his chin hairs. The tidbits now resided on my black jacket.

"Thanks," I said.

His ears swiveled toward me.

"I missed you, too."

He rubbed his slobbering muzzle on my coat sleeve and tried to knock the grain bucket from my hand. The more time I spent practicing with Charm, the more we missed each other when I was in class or studying. I rubbed his back in small circles the way he liked and lightly kneaded his neck with my knuckles. He grunted with pleasure.

A couple of stalls over, Callie fed Black Jack a few

mint candies she had swiped from the tin outside Mr. Conner's office. Jack had an insatiable sweet tooth and Callie occasionally indulged him with candy. Peppermint was his favorite treat.

"You coming?" I asked, stepping up to Jack's stall.

She eyed a tangle in Jack's dark mane. "I better get that out," she said. "See you tomorrow for our ride?"

"Absolutely," I said, passing Julia and Alison near the tack room door. They scowled at me, but didn't say a word.

I walked down to Mr. Conner's office. There, in the aisle, was the team trophy case. The wooden board with gold plaques glittered at me as I read the names of last year's advanced team. I put a finger on the cold glass.

"What are you doing here?" Julia asked, standing with her arms folded.

"I'm afraid I won't make it," I said truthfully. I expected Julia to laugh at me, but she didn't.

"We all are," she said. "The amount we practice, we should *all* make the team."

"You're a good rider," I said, not looking away from the case.

"You don't suck either," she said.

We laughed, and then stood in silence.

I closed my eyes and tried to imagine hearing Mr. Conner call my name for the advanced team. The word "congratulations" rolled around in my head. A smile crept over across my face.

When I opened my eyes, Julia was gone.

32

AND THE ADVANCED
TEAM IS . . .

GLOOMY SKIES HUNG OVER US AS CALLIE, Jack, Charm, and I headed down the trail toward Canterwood. The fat, gray clouds looked as though they'd burst over us at any minute. Charm shivered and I adjusted the blanket draped across his hindquarters. He skirted around a clump of mud, left over from a slushy sleet from last night, and nearly stepped off the trail into a patch of burrs. I pressed my left boot firmly into his side to get his attention. He chomped on the bit and tugged on the reins.

"What's his deal today?" Callie asked.

"He's been off since we started," I said, stroking Charm's neck. I guided him Western style, with the reins in my left hand.

Black Jack eyed Charm warily, as if afraid of getting a nip on the neck.

Charm had never bitten anyone or anything, but he was certainly moody today.

"He's nervous," Callie said. Jack tossed his head at Callie's voice.

Since we had started our ride twenty-five minutes earlier, Callie had chattered nonstop about what making the team would do for us and our stable status.

"Sorry, but I can't help it," she said. "When we get back, Mr. Conner is going to make the announcement. We have a real shot at this."

"There are a lot of good riders," I said.

Charm's gait quickened into an extended walk as we neared the stables. He probably sensed my jitters. The waiting we had endured this week had been an absolute killer, and the depressing weather hadn't helped much either.

By the time we got back to the stable, Charm was cool and didn't need to be walked. I untacked him and noticed Mike had filled his hay net and water bucket.

"Treat?" I asked.

Charm made a face that suggested I should have known the answer to my question. I stuck my hand in the plastic bag outside of his stall and offered him one of the apple-flavored cookies. He snatched it from my hand and devoured it in seconds, crumbs flying everywhere.

"Piggy," I laughed. With Charm still munching, I latched his stall and headed for the bathroom.

I leaned over the sink, splashing water on my face, and redid my ponytail. I smoothed a coat of my new tangerine lip gloss over my lips, but my stomach still felt queasy. *Yoga breathing*, I reminded myself.

I entered the meeting room off the arena and took a seat. Mr. Conner had the room draped in green and gold streamers and a six- or seven-foot banner said, CONGRATULATIONS CANTERWOOD CREST RIDERS! The tables were cloaked in white tablecloths and dotted with glasses of ginger ale in champagne flutes. A horseshoe-shaped cake with "Welcome New Teammates!" had green icing with tiny gold horses around the cake's edge.

"Nervous?" Sam asked. She was one of the lucky ones already on the advanced team.

"How did you stand the wait?" I asked back.

"I cleaned my dorm room from top to bottom, for a week straight. My roommate hated me because I wouldn't stop," she said.

I looked for Callie, but she wasn't here yet. Nicole,

sitting a few seats over, waved. Alison and Julia sat with arms crossed and matching glares. The newly formed "duo" looked lost without their ringleader. Aristocrat was still in his stall, but I hadn't seen Heather all day.

Callie came into the room and sat next to me.

"Where were you?" I whispered.

"Look!" she said, pointing toward the door.

Heather Fox.

Heather sashayed in front of the room and headed for her friends. A smug Julia removed her hobo purse and gave Heather a seat. They pushed their chairs closer and started chatting. My chances of team glory began to fade away.

"Why didn't you tell me?" I asked Callie.

"I just found out! I heard that she convinced her parents to let her stay."

We kept our eyes on Heather. The large wall clock in the room seemed to tick loud enough that each second echoed in my ears. Where was Mr. Conner? The man was never late.

Finally, the door creaked open and Mr. Conner stepped through. He carried two large cardboard boxes under his arm. One box was sealed with clear masking tape and the other was open and filled with papers. Mr. Conner took his time as he set the boxes on the table. He reached into the box and pulled out a few white papers.

The room was silent. All eyes were focused on Mr. Conner. This was it!

"Do you see our names?" Callie asked, her brown eyes wide.

"I can't read through paper!" I said.

I wondered, briefly, what Mr. Conner would he do if I ran up and snatched the papers out of his hands.

"Sorry to keep you all waiting," he said. "There were a few last-minute details that needed my attention. I know you're all anxious to hear the news. So, I won't drag this out. Let's get started."

"Good luck," Callie whispered.

"Good luck to both of us," I said.

"Just a reminder that I used several criteria in each of your evaluations," Mr. Conner said. "I chose members for the advanced team who met the highest standards of talent, responsibility, drive, and strong team relations. The advanced team will represent Canterwood at the leading equestrian competitions across the country."

He peered down at the papers.

"With great pleasure, I'm pleased to announce your new advanced team representatives."

A hush fell over the arena. No one moved. I reached over and took Callie's hand.

"Julia Myer," Mr. Conner called. His voice echoed in the small space as cheers and clapping erupted from the students. Heather and Alison stood and clapped their hands above their heads. Julia shook Mr. Conner's hand and took the paper. "Congratulations," Mr. Conner said.

"Thankyousomuch!" Julia said, spitting out her sentence. She danced back to her seat.

One slot gone. Four to go.

Mr. Conner took out the next piece of paper. "Our next addition to the team is Callie Harper!"

Callie turned to me with a dazed look. "Did he just say my name?"

"Yes," I said, shoving her out of her seat. "Get up there!"

Callie stepped up to Mr. Conner. She almost hugged him, but pulled herself back at the last minute. He grinned and patted her shoulder. The other students clapped as she floated back to her seat. I stood and whistled. Nicole, jumping up from her seat, clapped and yelled, "Go Callie!" Any tension Callie and I had over the past few weeks melted away. This was my friend and she'd just made the team.

Callie plopped back into the seat, carefully holding her paper.

Mr. Conner had three papers left. If I had worked harder in algebra, I probably could have figured my odds. Heather straightened and grabbed Julia and Alison's hands.

"The next member of your team is Alison Robb!" Two seats left. I tried to watch Mr. Conner's gaze to see if he was looking at me with pity or congratulations. But he was unreadable.

Alison let out a squeal and dashed up to Mr. Conner. With wide eyes, she took the paper. Julia welcomed her back with a hug, but their expressions morphed into frowns when they got a glimpse of Heather's glowering face.

"The next member of your team is," Mr. Conner said. *Oh, God, please say my name!* "Heather Fox!"

Squeals rang out from Heather's section when Mr. Conner announced her name. Julia and Alison stood and clapped.

Heather headed for Mr. Conner and stopped in front of him. She folded her hands politely and waited for him to reach for her hand. She looked relieved to be up there.

Mr. Conner shook her hand and Heather gave a little curtsy before heading back to her seat. Her smile couldn't have been wider.

"The final member of the team is," Mr. Conner said. I shut my eyes. Watching him was too hard. "Sasha Silver! Congratulations!"

Callie didn't wait for me to get up. She dragged me to my feet and let out a victory cheer. "You did it!" she yelled.

Oh. My. God. Omigod! Everything Charm and I worked for had paid off. The hours of muscle pounding practice, the squabbles with Heather, leaping over the jumps on the outdoor course—it was all worth it.

"I can't believe it!" I said. "I made it?" I tried not to trip on a chair as I made my way to Mr. Conner. The green and gold decorations seemed to glitter and glow.

When I reached Mr. Conner, I shook his hand and let out a sigh I felt I'd been holding in all semester. "Thank you, sir," I manage to utter. "I'm going to work really hard."

"Your group practice begins at seven the first week of January," he said with a genuine smile and a sparkle in his eye.

I collapsed into my chair and opened the folded white piece of paper.

Congratulations, Sasha! All of us at the Canterwood Riding Team welcome your addition. We hope you'll find continued success on the advanced team and we look forward to working and riding with you. Best, Canterwood Crest Academy Riding Team Staff

Totally frame worthy. Carefully, I stuck it inside my jacket pocket.

Peering around the Trio, I saw Nicole, biting her lip as her eyes filled with tears. She, like over three-fourths of the riders, had to test again next year. Poor Nicole. It could have just as easily have been me, Callie, or anyone else.

"To those of you who didn't make it, I highly encourage you to try again next year," Mr. Conner said. "You are all talented riders. Do *not* let this discourage you. To those who did make it," he said. "Congratulations. I know you'll do Canterwood Crest Academy proud."

Callie and I grinned at each other.

Mr. Conner cleared his throat. "Before we adjourn, I have one last announcement to make."

I looked at Callie. She shrugged and gripped her paper tighter.

"Over the past three months, it has been brought to my attention by several anonymous students that there have been some serious issues surrounding our riders."

Mr. Conner looked at all of us. I shifted in my seat and glanced down to avoid his gaze.

"Students have come to me with serious allegations of

sabotage and unnecessary emotional stress inflicted upon certain students."

Heather sat ramrod straight and didn't look at anyone.

Mr. Conner tilted his head down and leaned forward for emphasis. "This behavior is not acceptable for any team member—advanced team or not—and it will not be tolerated. Next semester, any rumors or suggestions of ill behavior toward other team members will be taken extremely seriously. Action *will* be taken against any student who is determined to be the cause of these issues."

Heather's face bloomed carnation pink.

Mr. Conner stepped back and nodded once at all of us. "That being said, let's get back to the reason for today and give a round of applause for our new advanced team." Everyone burst into applause. Nicole, smiling through her watery eyes, gave me a thumbs-up.

Mr. Conner smiled at us. "Everyone should grab a piece of cake. The new team members come with me."

While everyone else got in line for cake, Mr. Conner took us to a back table where it was quiet and set down the box. "Go ahead and open it," he said.

Callie pulled out her dorm keys and sliced open the box. She pulled back the cardboard flaps and reached under the white tissue paper. After she pulled out a handful of paper, we saw green and gold fabric.

"What is it?" Callie asked. She reached inside and pulled out a jacket. Not just any jacket, but a Canterwood one with *Silver* emblazoned on the back.

"Team jackets!" I said. I slipped on the jacket and looked down at the front. The gold stitching on the lapel read "Canterwood Crest Academy Riding Team." Just like the shirt Mr. Conner always wore.

Callie pulled another jacket out of the box. "I've got one, too!" She put her arms into the sleeves and twirled around. The back read *Harper* in the same fancy script as my jacket lettering.

"We look like a team now," I cheered.

Heather looked over Julia's shoulder as Callie and I made room for them around the table. "I guess we're a team now," Heather said.

Callie reached inside the box and handed the jacket bearing the name *Fox* to Heather. "We've got to act like a team, or we're not going to make it," Callie said.

"I'm in," Heather said.

Julia and Alison lifted their jackets from the box and soon the five of us were all sporting them. We really looked like a team.

The Trio headed for the door, but Julia turned around before she left the room. "Congratulations," she said, looking at Callie and me. "See you at the party."

33

CANTERWOOD

SASHA

"TIME?" I YELLED.

"Six thirty!" Paige said. "You're the party host, Sasha. You can't be late—that would be tacky."

"One sec." I needed a final mirror check before heading out. My hair was piled into a chignon that, according to Paige, made my cheekbones pop, and I wore a pale blue keyhole top paired with skinny jeans and a pair of Paige's black boots. Earlier, Paige had put her diamond studs in my ears, had done my makeup and had given me a new look for the party.

"I still don't know if Jacob is coming," I said. Secretly, I was kind of relieved that there was a chance he wasn't coming. I'd probably be awful at the whole dance-and-small-talk thing. Sure, I'd spent time with Jacob before, but not with the pressure of a dance looming over me. I wasn't even brave enough to ask him to come in person.

"You never know," Paige said.

I was impressed with Paige's handiwork. I felt fairytale-ish. Paige had given my lashes a light coat of mascara. She'd also talked me into trying a sparkly pink lip gloss with a matching sheer blush.

"Come here!" Paige called, looking out the window. "Looks like your party is going to be perfect."

I couldn't believe it. Snow! Large, thick snowflakes covered the sidewalk. It was coming down so fast I couldn't see more than a couple of yards ahead. On the sidewalk, a couple ran through the snow together.

"We need to change your hair and then you *have* to go," Paige said. She grabbed my hairbrush and started to dismantle my chignon.

"But my hair was fine!"

"Just let me fix it," she said. "It's not snow hair." She combed my hair straight and gave me a deep side part. "Perfect."

"Are you sure you don't want to walk over with me?"

"I can't," she said. "Five more minutes for my hair and then I need to grab the desserts out of the fridge."

"Do you need help?"

Paige shooed me out the door. "I don't have much to bring over. Go!"

The Winchester hallway was deserted. Annabella and Kristen's room was already dark since they had gone home yesterday.

A rush of cold air hit me when I opened the door. The old-fashioned street lamps lit the glittery ground. Snowflakes danced in the light from the lanterns. My boots crunched in the snow as I hurried to the stables. Mr. Conner had said he would unlock everything, turn on the lights and set out the food and drinks. Close to the stable, I heard the neigh of horses and the jingle of bells.

Mr. Conner had six of the stable's calmest, strongest horses hitched to six red, black, and silver sleighs. Jingle bells as big as grapefruits hung off the sleigh with smaller bells attached to harnesses and reins. A liver chestnut hitched to the first sleigh shook his mane and the bells rang across the yard. Hot air blew from the horses' nostrils and floated up to the sky. The stable glowed with a warm yellow light.

I ran to Charm's stall. "Hey, boy!" I said, peering at him over the door. He was asleep in the back of his stall with one hoof cocked comfortably. "I'd come in, but I can't get dirty. I'll see you after the party, okay?" Charm opened a sleepy eye and then let out a soft sigh. He was out for the night.

Students filled the arena. A few danced in the middle of the room, others lined up at the food tables and some chatted and laughed as they sat in the chairs. And I had worried I'd be the only one to show up! Even the chaperones looked like they were having a great time.

In the far corner of the room, by the big Christmas tree, stood the Trio. They smiled and giggled—it was nice to see everyone happy. I glanced around for Jacob, but didn't see him.

"Have you seen Sasha Silver?" Callie asked, grinning as she took my hand and twirled me in a circle.

"I really want to ride the sleighs," I said. "Let's go get one together."

"Snack first and then sleigh?" Callie suggested.

"Sounds good to me." As if on cue, Paige entered through a side door, her arms laden with covered dishes. Callie and I went over to help her.

"This looks fantastic, Sasha," Paige said as we set down the bowls, plates and tray. "Your *food* looks fantastic," I said. "Everyone's going to love it."

"They better," Paige said with a snort. She had gone all-out on cupcakes with snow-people faces, mini turkey sandwiches, and frozen strawberry desserts.

I looked over at Callie, who was too busy stuffing her face with a cookie to talk.

Mr. Conner had set the loud speaker to play holiday tunes. I wondered what dancing with Jacob would feel like. Would it be weird? I'd probably crush his toes or something. Oh, well, it didn't look like I was going to find out tonight.

"You should sit and relax for a while, now that all the planning is out of the way," I reminded Paige.

"Just as long as I can see people's faces," she said. "I'm going to take a poll on my cupcake and frosting recipe later." We sat and started to gobble the food.

More people came inside. Ollie and Becky, two of the team's ninth grade advanced riders, stopped in front of Paige, Callie, and me just as I stuffed my mouth with an almond cookie.

"We wanted to tell you what a great job you did!" Ollie exclaimed.

"Thanks!" I said. "Have you gone on a sleigh ride yet?"

"We're headed there now," Becky said. "See you later!" They walked off and I turned to Paige and Callie.

"Can you believe they talked to us?" I squealed. "Us? The lowly seventh graders?"

"You did an amazing job," Paige said.

We laughed and dug back into our strawberry frozen ice. Paige finished her dessert and headed for the
tables to check on the food. She pointed out her cupcakes to one of the riders and launched into a list of
every ingredient she put into it. The girl nodded, staring at Paige with wide eyes. Maybe Paige had found
an apprentice.

The Trio slid into the seats beside Callie and me. They
all had on matching black nail polish.

"What are you guys doing for Thanksgiving?" I asked
them.

Julia brightened and twirled a sapphire ring on her
finger. "My parents are taking my sister and me to my
aunt's house in L.A. We're having a big party and we got
three tofurkeys this year!"

"Toe-what?" Callie asked, giggling.

Julia laughed. "Tofurkeys. It's a tofu turkey."

"I'm going home for Thanksgiving," Alison said. "I
can't wait to sleep in my own bed and see my pugs."

Funny, I'd pegged her as a poodle girl.

"What about you?" Julia asked Callie.

"Home," Callie said. "I'm baking pumpkin pies with
my mom."

"That sounds like my Thanksgiving, minus the baking," I said.

Heather sat still and didn't offer up any plans.

"What are you doing?" Callie finally asked Heather.

Heather stared at her hands. "I'm going to my grandma's," she said, her tone clipped. "My parents are going to Hawaii."

"Sorry," I said. "That sucks."

Heather slumped in her seat. "Whatever."

It was weird to have even a sort-of conversation with Heather.

"Maybe they don't know you want to go," I said. "Could you call them or something?"

Heather shrugged and stared at me as if I had dared her. "Maybe." With that, she got up and left the arena.

Alison and Julia headed off after her.

"Look," Callie said. "By the door."

Jacob stood in the garland-covered doorway, scanning the room. Oh, my God, he came!

"What now?" I asked, trying to duck behind Callie. This whole boy/girl dance thing was nothing like it was on TV or the movies. Movies always made it look fun to approach a guy at a dance, but this was torture!

Callie pushed my arm. "Pretend that since you're

the hostess, you're supposed to greet everyone."

Okay. This was just Jacob.

Jacob waved.

"Hi," I said, when I reached him. *It's just Jacob*, I reminded myself. *You've played video games with him*. But he was still a boy at my party and I was the girl who had invited him.

Jacob glanced around at the room and grinned. "You did all of this?"

"Not by myself," I said, slipping back into a kind of easiness. "I had lots of help."

"It looks great," he said, stepping closer to me. "Do you want to, uh, dance or something?" A look of uncertainty flickered in his green eyes. Was *he* afraid I'd say no?

"Sure," I said slowly, trying not to panic about my dance skills that didn't exist.

We headed to the middle of the floor, and stood at arm's length from each other, until I finally stepped closer and he took my hands.

We swayed together to the music—a slow song, thank God! But every movement felt awkward.

"Oops," I said, stepping on his foot. My face flamed with embarrassment.

"Doesn't the guy usually step on the girl's feet?" he joked.

"Are you going home tomorrow?" I asked.

"Yeah, it'll be a traditional Schwartz Thanksgiving—football and way too much food."

Twenty minutes later, we had danced through several songs, including a really bad rap version of "Jingle Bells," when Jacob touched my elbow. "Do you want to keep dancing?"

I looked over and saw Callie talking to Paige. She gave me a thumbs up.

"Definitely," I said.

I swallowed hard when "Silent Night" started to filter softly over the loudspeakers. A slow song. Oh, my God.

Jacob held out his right hand and I placed my hand in his. I hoped mine wasn't gross and sweaty.

Jacob moved his other hand to my waist and I tried to remember what to do with my free hand. I looked around and got my answer. Shoulder.

Jacob looked at me and smiled. I tried not to look as if I'd never danced like this before. We started to sway to the music and with every line, I relaxed. I hadn't melted into a puddle of embarrassment and Jacob didn't hate slow dancing with me. This was turning into the perfect night!

We danced through a few more songs before Jacob glanced at his watch.

"I should head back and finish packing," he said. "But I had a really great time. Thanks for inviting me."

"I had fun, too," I said.

Jacob pulled a piece of paper out of his pocket and handed it to me and I remembered when we'd gone for ice cream and he'd handed me his IM name.

"My cell number," he said. "You know, in case you want to talk over break or something."

"Cool," I said. All I could do was smile.

"Okay," he said, grinning. "See you soon."

He turned and headed out of the room and I watched him look back at me before he closed the door.

I, Sasha Silver, had just survived my first dance with a boy. Sure, I had stepped on his feet a couple of times and yes, I had been nervous. But I'd danced anyway—and lived to tell the tale. Apparently, that's what Canterwood Sasha did.

34

HEATHER'S CONFESSION

"YOU GUYS WERE SO CUTE TOGETHER," CALLIE said. "He wanted to dance with you all night." She adjusted her snowflake earrings.

Livvie made her way over, looking happy and party-ready in a sparkly white sweater and black jeans.

"I have to get back to the dorm in a minute, but I wanted to stop by and see this," Livvie said. "The decorations are amazing!"

"Thanks," I said.

"It was definitely worth all the hard work you girls put into it," she said.

"Before you go, you should grab one of Paige's cupcakes," I said, pointing to the food table. "But don't ask her about the recipe unless you have an hour to kill."

Laughing, Livvie waved and headed over to Paige.

"Time for a sleigh ride!" Callie said. We'd stuffed our-selves with more cookies, linked arms, and stepped outside into the real Winter Wonderland. Snow fell gently in fat flakes. The horses shook it off their backs and out of their manes.

"It's gorgeous," I whispered, my breath visible in the air. We headed for an empty sleigh, our footsteps crunching in the snow. The lanterns lit up the endless fences behind us.

We stepped up to the sleigh. My fingers couldn't resist touching a golden jingle bell.

"You first," I said.

Callie climbed into the black sleigh and I gave the gray horse a quick pat on the flank.

I gripped the sleigh and climbed inside.

"Sasha!" It was Heather, wrapped in her long black coat, snowflakes whitening her shoulders.

"What's up?" I asked. We stood in silence for a moment. We were close enough that our visible breaths clashed in the air.

"Thanks," she said. "For being so nice to me after

everything." Heather shoved her hands into her coat pockets. "I also wanted to apologize." She stopped and looked up at the night sky. "I'm sorry."

"If we can't act like a team, we'll all lose," I said.

"I don't like to lose," Heather said, swiping a long strand of hair off her face.

"That makes two of us," I said.

She paused. "You should also know that I followed Callie into Winchester and took her note. The one where she asked you to practice with her."

Behind me, one of the horses rattled the jingle bells and let out an impatient neigh. A chilly wind picked up and made us pull our coats tighter.

I adjusted my gloves. "We're teammates now," I said, looking at Heather. "Friends" was the wrong word.

Heather nodded.

"Have a good Thanksgiving," I said, and walked back to the sleigh.

The driver who was dressed in a black coat, top hat and white gloves helped me into the sleigh. Callie handed me a thick, checkered blanket to cover our laps. The driver clicked to the horse and the sleigh lurched forward over the snow. Heather stood there as we pulled away—getting smaller and smaller.

The driver aimed for the snow-covered woods. Lanterns dotted the trail and gave off a gentle yellow glow. The horse's bells jingled. The trees looked soft and cottony. I wished the ride could go on forever. I wrapped the red and green checkered blanket tighter around my legs and warmed my hands underneath.

Callie bumped her shoulder against mine. "Here's to Canterwood!"

"Here's to the advanced team!" I said.

I couldn't wait. Going home would be nice, but coming back to Canterwood would be even better. And this time, Charm and I wouldn't get spooked.